The Audience Goes Wild for
CHORUS LINES, CAVIAR, AND CORPSES
The First *Happy Hoofers* Mystery

"The Happy Hoofers bring hilarity and hijinks to the high seas—or in this case, a Russian River Cruise where murder is nothing to tap at. The cruise finds them kick-ball-changing and flap-kicking their way across Russia on a ship where murder points to more than a few unusual suspects."
—**Nancy Coco**, author of *All Fudged Up*

"A page-turning cozy mystery about five friends in their 50's, dancing their way across Russia. From the first chapter, McHugh delivers. . . . The cast of characters includes endearing, scary, charming, crazy, and irresistible people. Besides murder and mayhem, we are treated to women who we might want as our best friends, our shrinks, and our travel companions."
—**Jerilyn Dufresne**, author of the Sam Darling
   mystery series

"*Spasiba*, Mary McHugh——that's Russian for 'thank you.' *Chorus Lines, Caviar, and Corpses* is a huge treat for armchair travelers and mystery fans alike, as five spirited tap-dancers cruise from St. Petersburg to Moscow undeterred by a couple of shipboard murders. Vivid description and deft touches of local color take the reader right along with them."
—**Peggy Ehrhart**, author of the Maxx Maxwell
   mystery series

"A fun book! Mary McHugh's *Chorus Lines, Caviar, and Corpses* is, quite literally, a romp. It has a little bit of everything, from tongue-in-cheek travel tips to ro-

mance and recipes (and oh, are they *good*.). Not even the most jaded reader will be able to resist plucky Tina Powell and her cadre of capering cougars aboard a cruise ship where death is on the menu, along with the caviar. What could be more delicious?"
—**Carole Bugge**, author of *Who Killed Blanche DuBois?*

"If you can't afford a Russian cruise up the Volga, this charming combination murder mystery travelogue, which mixes tasty cuisine and a group of frisky, wisecracking, middle-aged chorines, is the next best thing."
—**Charles Salzberg**, author of the Shamus Award
  nominee *Swann's Last Song*

Also by Mary McHugh

Flamenco, Flan, and Fatalities

Mary McHugh

KENSINGTON PUBLISHING CORP.
www.kensingtonbooks.com

KENSINGTON BOOKS are published by

Kensington Publishing Corp.
119 West 40th Street
New York, NY 10018

All Kensington Titles, Imprints, and Distributed Lines are available at special quantity discounts for bulk purchases for sales promotions, premiums, fund-raising, and educational or institutional use.

Special book excerpts or customized printings can also be created to fit specific needs. For details, write or phone the office of the Kensington special sales manager: Kensington Publishing Corp., 119 West 40th Street, New York, NY 10018, attn: Special Sales Department, Phone: 1-800-221-2647.

Kensington and the K logo Reg. U.S. Pat & TM Off.

ISBN-13: 978-1-61773-361-1
ISBN-10: 1-61773-361-X
First Kensington Mass Market Edition: March 2015

eISBN-13: 978-1-61773-362-8
eISBN-10: 1-61773-362-8
First Kensington Electronic Edition: March 2015

10 9 8 7 6 5 4 3 2 1

Printed in the United States of America

To Karen, Doug, Alex, Ian, and Michael, whom I love immoderately

Chapter 1

Buen Apetito!

I must say the five of us were a good-looking group in our silky summer dresses and strappy high heels, earrings swinging, as we strolled toward the coach that would take us to the restaurant for the first dinner on our tour of northern Spain. We climbed aboard and said hello to the other passengers from our luxury train. We couldn't wait to see everything, do everything, experience everything in this amazing country. We took seats in two available rows and craned our necks, looking out the windows at the bustling street in front of the station.

Just as the door closed and the driver gunned the engine into life, there was a loud commotion. We heard a familiar voice demanding that the bus wait for him. I looked out and saw a large, sweaty man waving his arms and shouting.

"Where is Eduardo?" he yelled. "He was supposed to make all the arrangements for me on the train. Where is he?"

I'd heard this voice before somewhere. A strong wave of dislike grabbed me. Who was this person? Why didn't I like him?

"Nobody knows how to do anything in this country," he said.

Eduardo, the host of our trip, got off the bus and held out his hand to the noisy man.

"I'm so sorry, Mr. Shambless. I'm Eduardo. We waited for you and your party as long as we could. We have reservations for dinner and we need to leave on time." Our host was slender and dapper in dark slacks and a starched white shirt. The shouter, by contrast, looked like an unmade bed.

"I'm filming this whole trip on your crowded little train for my TV show. I'd have thought you'd have the decency to wait for me and my crew before you ran off to the restaurant. They'll wait for us. They can't buy publicity like my show will give them. And neither can you." He waved a pudgy finger in Eduardo's face as if he were not the center of attention already.

"We are indeed grateful that you chose our trip, Mr. Shambless," Eduardo said. I cringed watching this nice man having to apologize to this creep. "I regret any confusion I may have caused. Please join us on the bus and tell me what I can do to help you."

"Just stay out of my way unless I need you,"

Shambless said, motioning to his cameraman and a pretty young woman with long, straight blond hair and a V-necked blouse that showed off her incredible breasts every time she bent over, which was often.

I remembered why I disliked this man. Dick Shambless was a television talk show host who enthralled whole sections of the country every day with his anti-gay, anti-government, anti-everything rantings. Why did he have to come on this trip?

One of the women sitting near us stood up and pulled the man sitting next to her to a seat in the back of the coach. I heard her say, "I don't want to talk to him," as she moved to the last row.

"Just ignore him, Sylvia," the man said, following her down the aisle with a camera bag over his shoulder. "You don't have to be afraid of him anymore."

I nudged my friend Mary Louise, who was leafing through a brochure about local attractions.

"Did you see the look on that woman's face when she heard Shambless's voice?" I whispered to her.

She looked up, concern in her lovely blue eyes. "She seemed—, I don't know,—angry? Scared? What was it?"

"Well, she certainly wasn't happy to see him."

The talk show host lurched onto the bus,

heaving his vast weight into the front seat, without a "hello" or "how are you" to anybody around him. The cameraman stood in the front of the bus and filmed Shambless, and then swung the camera around to include the rest of us.

Eduardo leaned over closer to Shambless, and said, "You might want to include our beautiful dancers who are going to entertain us on this trip. Our Happy Hoofers."

"Happy Hookers?" Shambless said. "Why would I want to include a bunch of hookers?"

"No, no," Eduardo said, embarrassed, looking at us apologetically. "They're dancers and we are really lucky to have them."

"Tell them to stand up," Shambless said. "Let me get a look at these babes."

Eduardo asked each of us to stand. We reluctantly got to our feet as he introduced us individually. I was ready to slug Shambless, but I felt sorry for Eduardo, so I smiled into the camera when he said, "This is Gini Miller, award-winning filmmaker and dancer extraordinaire."

Eduardo asked Tina to stand next. "And this is Tina Powell, magazine editor and leader of the dancers."

Shambless snorted when Eduardo motioned to Janice to stand. "Janice Rogers, actress and director," Eduardo said.

"You sure that's hoofers with an *f* ?" Shambless said.

I was about to punch his lights out when the

man with Sylvia called out, "Janice! Janice Rogers. I didn't know you were on this trip."

He pushed his way up the aisle to hug her.

"Janice Rogers," he said. "I don't believe you're here. It's so good to see you again. How are you? Are you still acting?"

Janice pulled away to look at him.

"Tom Carson," she said. "It must be ten years since we were in *Who's Afraid of Virginia Woolf?* in New York. How are you? Are you still acting?"

"If you can call it that. I'm in a soap opera. I haven't been in anything on the stage in years."

"Listen, there's nothing wrong with soaps. It's still acting. Which one are you in?"

"*Love in the Afternoon,*" he said. "Have you ever seen it?"

"I have, actually," she said. "In fact, it's really good. I got hooked on it one year when I didn't have an acting job and was just sitting around waiting for the phone to ring."

"I can't believe you ever sat around waiting for a part," Tom said. "You're a terrific actress."

"Can we get on with this?" Shambless said impatiently. "You can sleep with her later."

I would have killed him right then and there, but Tom said, "Let's catch up at dinner, Jan." Then he went back to his seat.

Eduardo introduced Pat as a family therapist and Mary Louise as "the mother of three," and the cameraman finished filming us.

As the bus started, the nicely stacked blonde

sat down next to Shambless and turned on a tape recorder. He started to talk into it when a petite woman behind him leaned over his seat, and said, "Oh, Mr. Shambless, I'm one of your biggest fans. I watch you every day and I thank God for all you do to protect our country. You're a national treasure."

He turned to her with a forced smile, and said, "God bless you. I'd be nothing without loyal fans like you." He patted her hand.

I felt like I was going to be sick, but I swallowed my bile and muttered to Pat sitting in front of me, "What is he doing here? He'll ruin the whole trip."

Pat turned around to say to me in a low voice, "We don't have to talk to him. In fact, please keep me from saying anything to him. He's a Neanderthal. He hates everything—intelligent women, gays, the president, social welfare programs—everything. I can never understand why so many people listen to him."

"I don't get that either," I said. "The few times I've heard him when I surf through the channels, I just wanted to strangle him."

"You'd make a lot of people happy if you did. Anyway, try to relax. Just ignore him and enjoy the ride."

"You're right, Pat, but it won't be easy."

On the way to the restaurant, our guide, a young Spanish woman named Rafaela, stood up and picked up a microphone to give us a brief history of this part of Spain, or Green Spain, as the northern section is called.

"Our train follows the five-hundred-mile route that pilgrims take from San Sebastian in the east to the cathedral in Santiago de Compostela in the west where the bones of St. James are buried—only we're going in the opposite direction. The legend is that St. James's body was brought from Jerusalem to Santiago de Compostela and buried in a field. Then nine hundred years later, someone found the bones and the cathedral was built around them. Pilgrims make the long journey to see them and are given a free room and meals when they arrive. If they make the pilgrimage when St. James Day falls on a Sunday, it's a holy year and all their sins are forgiven forever. They go directly to heaven."

"What a load of baloney," Shambless said. "You'd have to be a real idiot to believe that stuff. How far is this restaurant anyway? I'm starving."

The whole coach fell into a silence so hostile you could touch it.

Rafaela looked at him, her dark eyes reflecting the anger most people in the bus were feeling. With admirable restraint, she said, "It's only a short distance. In fact, you can see it up the road there on the right."

I stood up to peer out the front window of the coach and saw a startlingly white stucco hacienda, surrounded by brilliant red oleander flowers, which were even more beautiful against the stark restaurant walls. The September sun glinted off the sparkling windows. I could see a sign that read, BIENVENIDOS EL GUSTO DEL MAR, which I think means "Welcome to the Taste of the Sea." My Spanish isn't all that great.

When the bus pulled up to the gleaming white restaurant, Eduardo got off to shake hands with the owner, who was waiting to greet us. He was tall and handsome in the way that only Spanish men are—with that look in their eyes that says, "You cannot resist me."

"Ladies and gentlemen," Eduardo said, "I am pleased to introduce you to Señor Delgardo, the owner of El Gusto del Mar, this excellent restaurant."

Señor Delgardo smiled and held out his hand to Shambless, who was the first one to clamber out of the bus. The cameraman took pictures of the restaurant and the other buildings nearby. The blonde ignored the rest of us and put her arm through the talk show host's arm.

"*Bienvenido,* señor," Señor Delgardo said to him as he got off the bus. Shambless just grunted and pushed past him into the restaurant.

The rest of us tried to make up for his rudeness by shaking hands with the owner and telling him how much we were looking forward to dining in his restaurant. He worked at being gracious, but it was obvious that he felt insulted by Shambless's boorishness. Somehow, we were all crass Americans because of the thoughtlessness of the talk show host.

As we got off the bus, I noticed that Sylvia put her hand on her companion's arm to restrain him. I heard him say, "Don't be silly, Sylvia. It was a long time ago. Come on. You don't have to talk to him."

She followed him reluctantly into the restaurant.

Rafaela ushered us into a gleaming dark wood bar with a magnificent view of the beach and the Cantabrian Sea through the floor-to-ceiling windows. The white damask-covered tables were set with gleaming silver, crystal wine glasses, red and pink roses, and white candles. Most of the tables were reserved for our group of fifty passengers.

Shambless, still loud and obnoxious, sat down at a table for four and waved away other people who tried to sit with him, except for the blonde and the cameraman. "This is my vacation. I talk to people all year long. I don't want to bother with anybody while I'm eating," he said to Señor Delgardo when he tried to seat some of the passengers at his table.

The blonde whispered something in his ear and he smiled into the camera.

"Edit that out," he said to the camera operator. His voice changed into a mellow, pleasing baritone. "What a pleasure it is to be here in sunny Spain . . . what is it, Julie?"

She said something to him and he continued,

even more mellifluously than before. "Or, I should say rainy Spain," he said, a slight chuckle in his voice, "because it's the rain here in northern Spain that makes this Green Spain, a lush and beautiful place to see. I want to take you with me on this trip through picturesque fishing villages, to ninth-century monuments, to the Guggenheim museum. We'll climb mountains, watch the ocean splash on the shore, visit historic caves." He paused and smiled into the camera. "I'm so glad you're here with me on this fascinating journey."

He motioned to the cameraman to stop. "That's it for now, Steve," he said in his regular, ordinary, bossy voice. "Get some shots of the restaurant and the town around here."

He turned to Julie. "How was I, honey?"

She took his hand.

"Superb, as always."

He pulled his hand away and tore off a piece of bread from the basket on the table.

Our group was at the table next to his. We did our best to ignore him.

He looked up as the woman who was trying to avoid him and Tom, her companion, passed his table.

"Well," he said loudly. "It's been a long time, Sylvia. How's your life going? Still with that soap opera? *Lust in the Afternoon,* isn't it?"

Sylvia stiffened, stopped and looked at him with such hatred we could feel its heat, and then walked past him to a table as far from his as she could find. Tom glared at the talk show host and followed her to the back of the room.

"I wonder what that's all about?" Tina said.

Janice leaned forward, and in a low voice said, "Tom's a great guy. We were in a play together in New York a few years ago." She paused for a minute, a dreamy look on her face. "We had a little thing going for a while," she said. "Anyway, I heard that he married the producer of Shambless's talk show, a woman named Sylvia something or other. I don't know what happened exactly, but she left or was fired. I heard rumors that Shambless had her fired because she wouldn't sleep with him, and then kept her from being hired as a producer on other talk shows. That's how she ended up producing a soap opera. She hired Tom and I guess that's when they fell in love and got married. I had no idea he was on this trip."

"Hmm," I said. "Shambless makes friends wherever he goes."

We laughed and looked at Rafaela, who was about to tell us our dinner choices.

"Since this part of Spain is famous for its incredibly fresh seafood," she said, "the owner of this restaurant has selected the most delicate and delicious dishes." She translated the menu for us.

"Everything is superb here," she said. "You can have *cigalas cocidas,* which is boiled crayfish with

11

lemon wedges. The crayfish is so fresh it almost sings in your mouth."

"Oh, great," Shambless growled. "That's all I need—singing fish. I just want a steak, medium rare, with French fries. And a bottle of red wine, if they have any good wine in Spain. Think you can manage that?"

Señor Delgardo, who was standing nearby, looked at Rafaela. They didn't say anything, but their feelings about this man were unmistakable.

Obviously exerting a great effort to keep his voice pleasant, the owner said, "Señor Shambless, we are noted for our seafood. Try our *vieiras al horno,* which is—"

"Some kind of horny fish," Shambless said, snickering and looking at his fan at the next table, who giggled.

"As I said before," he said. "All I want is a steak. It's simple. A steak. Medium rare. With French fries. And ketchup."

Steve, the guy with the camera, leaned over Shambless and whispered something in his ear.

"Oh . . . yeah . . . good point. Wait a sec, Delgardo. Bring me one of your fish dishes with all the trimmings so Steve can film it for the documentary. And then bring me the steak."

Señor Delgardo turned abruptly and went into the kitchen.

Rafaela tried to pretend she hadn't heard all this and continued talking to the rest of us.

"As Señor Delgardo was saying, *vieiras al horno* is baked scallops. Again, very simple. Scallops made with onions, garlic, paprika, sprinkled with bread crumbs, fried, and then put in the oven briefly to brown the crumbs. They are fresh, fresh, fresh."

"Oh, blah, blah, blah," said Shambless. "Can you be more boring? I don't care what's on the friggin' menu. Bring it. Let Steve get a picture of it and then bring me my steak, if you can manage such a complicated order."

I'd had enough. "Well, we care, Shambless," I said. "So stuff a sock in it until your steak comes."

He turned slowly and looked me up and down, and then around the table at the rest of us.

"Ah, the dancing lesbians, I presume," he said, loudly enough for everyone in the restaurant to hear.

Tina put her hand on my arm, but I'd had enough. I jumped up and confronted him.

"Ah, the impotent talk show host, I presume," I said. I know it wasn't devastating and brilliant, but it was all I could think of at the moment.

"Gini, let it go," Pat said, pulling me back into my seat.

I sat back down, shaking, and looked at Rafaela, who rolled her eyes and told us the rest of our choices.

There was *salpicon,* a seafood salad, *calamari a la plancha,* a very spicy squid dish made with lots of hot red pepper flakes, and *bogavante a la gal-*

lega, which I ordered after finding out it was lobster and potatoes.

Each of us chose a different main course so we could trade bites to taste a variety of the tempting dishes on the menu. We were enjoying every mouthful and trying not to hear Shambless only a few feet away complaining to the chef, who had left the kitchen to find out what was wrong. Shambless complained that his steak was thin and overcooked and inedible.

"It tastes like horsemeat," he said.

This was too much for the chef, a red-faced, portly man, who looked like he would explode. He was about to say something, but the owner quickly led him back to the kitchen and then returned to say to Shambless, "Seafood is the specialty in this part of Spain, señor. Just try these scallops. I think you'll like them."

Shambless glowered at him, shoved the steak aside, and picked up one of the scallops on his fork. He didn't say anything, but he finished every one of them down to the last bite, and we were grateful his mouth was full.

As he was pouring his third glass of wine, his devoted fan came over and stood at his elbow. She was a small woman with short gray hair and a lumpy body. She shifted from leg to leg, smoothed her hair, pushed her glasses back on her nose, cleared her throat, and finally tapped him on the shoulder.

He looked up, annoyed at first, but when he saw that it was his adoring fan, he dredged up a pleasant expression, if not quite a smile.

"Yes, my dear, what can I do for you?"

"I don't mean to bother you, Mr. Shambless," she said, speaking rapidly, "but I just had to tell you how much I enjoy your show. You've taught me so much in the last ten years. I can't wait to tell my friends I met you on this trip. They all think you're wonderful too. We talk about you all the time. So I was wondering, could I trouble you for your autograph? I want them all to know I really met you."

Shambless paused in midbite and said, his mouth full, "Of course, dear lady. I'm always glad to oblige one of my viewers. Let me sign your menu. What's your name, sweetheart?"

"Dora. Dora Lindquist. Thank you. This means so much to me. I live alone and your show is my best friend."

Julie got up and picked up her purse, which I noticed was a Coach. "I'm going to the—what do they call it?—the señoritas' room. I'll be back when no one is bothering you."

Dora looked up and watched her walk to the restroom. For a minute her face was serious, but she quickly regained her eager expression when she looked back at Shambless.

He bent over the menu Dora offered him, wrote a message, and then signed it. He took her hand. "It's always a pleasure to meet one of my viewers," he said.

She giggled nervously and held the menu close against her chest.

"What a beautiful ring," he said, still holding her hand. "It's like a locket. How unusual."

"Yes, it has a picture of my little girl in it. She was very beautiful."

"*Was* beautiful?

Dora looked away from him for a minute and I could see that she was trying not to cry. She started to speak and then her voice broke.

"She . . . she . . . died. Last year. She was very sick."

"I'm so sorry to hear that," Shambless said, dropping her hand and slathering a piece of bread with butter. "Could I see her picture?"

Dora backed away and started to return to her table.

"Oh, no. I'm interrupting your dinner. I don't want to bother you."

"It's no bother. I'd like very much to see her picture." He took another swallow of wine.

"No, no, that's all right," Dora said, moving away from him. "I'll show it to you another time. Please finish your dinner. And thank you."

"It is I who should thank you," he said, pouring himself another glass of wine.

Shambless motioned to the photographer.

"Did you get that, Steve?" he said. "I want a lot of footage of my adoring fans."

"Yeah, I got it," Steve said. "The whole thing."

After she went back to her table, Shambless looked over at us, and said, "Hey, dancers, you could take a few lessons in femininity from that sweet woman who asked for my autograph. That's how a lady acts. But look whom I'm talking to."

I could not stay silent this time either. I was afraid I'd burst a blood vessel if I did.

"Any one of us is more woman than you can handle, Shambless," I said. "Whatever happened to your three wives, by the way? Didn't they act like ladies?"

Tina tugged at my sleeve, and said out of the corner of her mouth, "Let him alone, Gini. He's not worth it."

"How can you just sit there and let that idiot say those things, Tina?" I said angrily. "What's the matter with you?"

Pat, sitting next to me, looked up, and said quietly, "How many desserts do you think he can eat?"

This made me laugh. I sat down and let my anger go. God bless Pat. I could always count on her to make me stop making a fool of myself. The others all took a deep breath and relaxed.

"Sorry, guys," I muttered. "I'll be good. But that man drives me crazy."

Shambless attacked the rest of his dinner and

wine greedily, looking up briefly as the blonde sat down next to him again. She picked at her food and then leaned closer to him and said something that annoyed him.

"I told you we'll talk about that later," he said, loud enough for us to hear. "Stop asking me about it. I'll take care of it when the time is right."

"You keep saying that," she said, her voice getting louder. "But the time is never right. I'm sick of waiting. You have to do something about it now."

"I don't have to do anything," he said, his voice even louder. "Don't tell me what to do. I told you I'd take care of this and I will. But leave me alone or you'll be on the next plane home."

She took a sip of her wine and ate a few more bites of her dinner. Then she stood up, threw her napkin on the table, and said to him, "I've had enough. I'll wait outside until it's time to go back to the train." She left the table and the dining room.

Shambless ignored her and kept on eating and drinking.

He looked up as Sylvia and Tom passed his table on their way out.

"Had enough to eat, Sylvia? Wouldn't want to get fat. They might kick you out of show business." He laughed nastily.

Tom tried to stop her, but Sylvia came close to the talk show host, leaned over next to him, and in a voice filled with hatred, said to him, "I've had more than enough, Dick. Keep your rotten comments to yourself or you'll be very sorry."

"What are you going to do, get your own talk show?" Shambless said with a smirk.

"I'm going to do more than talk," Sylvia said, and Tom pulled her away.

"Forget it, Syl," he said. "He's not worth it."

She straightened up and let Tom lead her out of the restaurant.

We sat there stunned, bowled over by Sylvia's emotion.

Shambless looked up from his dinner, and said, "What are you staring at, hookers? Try minding your own business for a change."

Rafaela came over to our table before I could explode again.

"You have to have one of our desserts," she said, putting her hand on my shoulder. "They are divine. We have strawberries with whipped cream, almond tart, chocolate tart, and my favorite, tiramisu, even if it is Italian."

We all groaned. "Rafaela, tiramisu is my favorite dessert," Janice said, "but if we eat one more thing we won't be able to walk, much less dance tonight."

She laughed. *"Muy bien,"* she said. "I won't tempt you. But did you enjoy your dinner?"

We all talked at once trying to tell her how delicious the food was, how beautiful the restaurant was, how much we enjoyed being there.

"Rafaela," Mary Louise said, "I don't mean to be a pest, but is there any chance you could get the recipes for the seafood salad, the calamari, and the lobster? I would love to make them when I get home."

"Let me see what I can do," Rafaela said, and went into the kitchen.

We were interrupted by loud talk from the next table. I heard Shambless say to Eduardo, "I must have a car take me back to the train. I can't ride in that crowded coach again."

"I'm so sorry, señor, but there are no cars available now. I'm afraid you'll have to ride in the bus with the rest of us. It's only a short distance."

Shambless glared at him. "I'm not used to riding on buses," he said contemptuously. "Do something about it. You're in charge here."

Eduardo took the owner aside and spoke to him rapidly in Spanish. The owner nodded.

Eduardo came back to Shambless. "You are in luck. Señor Delgardo, our host, said he would drive you back to the train."

"I hope his driving is better than his food," Shambless said.

He looked up as we passed his table on our way out. "Aren't you girls a little old to be dancing on trains?" he said.

Tina shot me a warning glance, but I couldn't help it. "Aren't you a little fat for a narrow-gauge track?" I said.

My friends dragged me back to the bus before he could answer, but I was still fuming. One woman from the train stopped, smiled at me, and patted my arm as she got back on the bus. "Don't pay any attention to him," she said with a French accent. "He's obnoxious."

"I could kill him," I said. "He's spoiling this whole experience."

As we climbed aboard the bus, we could see Shambless getting into the owner's car. It was a small car and he was a very big man. Steve and the driver pushed and pulled him into the car and closed the door.

When we were all on the bus again, Rafaela came running up, and climbed aboard, and walked up the aisle to Mary Louise.

"Here are those recipes you asked for," she said, handing her some loose pages. "Enjoy."

"You're an angel, Rafaela," Mary Louise said. "Thank you so much."

Back on the train, we were all feeling way too well-fed and not at all sure we could fit into the long, tight-fitting dresses that were slit up the sides so our legs were free to move, stamp, kick, and bend, flamenco style. Covered with silver sequins, they were pure glitter and flash. I loved wearing my gown because it was the total opposite of my usual costume of a T-shirt and jeans.

I was sharing a suite with Tina.

She struggled with her gown.

"Gini, give me a hand with this zipper, will you?" Tina said. "I think I gained a couple of pounds back there at that restaurant."

"Our dance tonight should use up a few thousand calories," I said.

"Olé!" Tina said, clicking her heels and moving in a tiny circle in our crowded room. "Ready, Gini?"

"Olé!" I said, opening the door.

We grabbed our scarves and knocked on the door of our friends' suite.

Our three partners were silver-sequined and gorgeous.

"Are we the best or what?" Janice said.

"We're certainly the best fed," Mary Louise said, patting her stomach. "I'm feeling a little stuffed."

"We all are," Tina said, "But we'll be fine once we get on that floor and start moving. Come on, all together now, think flamenco, think clapping hands and flashing feet."

We headed for the ballroom car, waving at the other passengers as we passed through the cars. The ballroom somehow looked smaller than it did in the afternoon.

"Shouldn't we have rehearsed in this car before we actually performed here?" Pat, our worrier, said.

"We'll be okay, Pat," Tina said. "We dance in and out of each other, not in a straight line. We can do it."

Tina clicked on the CD player and the first notes of the flamenco music filled the air.

Just as we were ready to swing out onto the floor, Eduardo ran up to us. He looked frantic, not his usual cool, dignified self.

"Señoras, I have terrible news." He stopped, tried to calm down.

"What's the matter, Eduardo?" Tina asked, touching his arm. "What has happened?"

He took a deep breath. "He's dead," he said. "He's . . ."

"Who's dead, Eduardo?" I asked. "What are you talking about?"

"Señor Shambless," he said. "His room attendant, Carlos, found him a half hour ago. He was a mess. Carlos called me and I called Dr. Parnell, one of our passengers. He examined Señor Shambless and confirmed that he was dead. I called the police and they are on their way here now."

"Oh, Eduardo, what can we do to help you?" Tina asked.

He looked at us, pleading. "I know it's a terrible thing to ask, señoras, but could you please dance anyway? I don't want the other passengers to know what has happened just yet, and your dancing will keep them here while I figure out what to do."

We looked at each other, straightened up, nodded yes, and told Eduardo not to worry. We would distract the audience or wear out our dancing shoes trying.

MARY LOUISE'S ADAPTATION OF THE RESTAURANT RECIPES

Salpicon de Marisco (Seafood Salad)

1 lb shrimp, cooked, peeled, and deveined
1 lb cooked crabmeat, cut up
1 lb cooked octopus or squid, cut up
1 red bell pepper, cut up
1 green bell pepper, cut up
1 cup small white onions, left whole
1 medium yellow onion, sliced
1 cup gherkin pickles, halved
1 cup green olives stuffed with anchovies and
  left whole

Dressing:
4 tbsp. white vinegar
8 tbsp olive oil
Salt and pepper to taste

Mix the seafood together in a large bowl and add next six ingredients.

Whisk white vinegar and olive oil together in small bowl to make dressing. Season with salt and pepper to taste.

Pour dressing over salad and toss. Serve at room temperature.

Serves six.

Calamari a la Plancha (Spicy Squid)

⅓ cup olive oil
1½ lb raw calamari rings
4 cloves garlic, minced
1½ tbsp chopped parsley
¼ tsp red pepper flakes
Sea salt to taste
4 lemon wedges

Heat olive oil to sizzling in large skillet. Saute calamari for about three minutes and then add minced garlic. (I use four cloves, but you can use more if you like really garlicky calamari.) Cook until the calamari is golden brown and the garlic smells great but isn't too brown, about seven minutes. Be careful not to let calamari get rubbery. Add chopped parsley and red pepper flakes. Add some sea salt and garnish with lemon wedges and serve immediately.

Serves four.

Bogavante a la Gallega (Galician Lobster with Potatoes)

2 medium-sized potatoes, boiled and diced
2 3-lb. boiled lobsters
2 tbsps salt
Sweet Spanish paprika to taste
3 oz. olive oil
2 bay leaves
Black pepper to taste

Keep potatoes warm. When lobster is room temperature, detach tails from lobster and put one on each plate. Using a sharp knife, take meat out of tails, slice, and put back in tails.

Crack open claws with a nutcracker and remove meat with a cocktail fork. Arrange claw meat and potatoes around tails and sprinkle sweet Spanish paprika, salt and ground black pepper over all. Add salt and olive oil and enjoy.

Serves two.

Gini's photography tip: Ask permission before you shoot someone in a foreign country—either with your camera or a gun.

Chapter 2

And Your Name Is?

We started the music over again. The flamenco music set the mood of excitement. It was gypsy music from southern Spain. Guitar music started low and slow, and built to a climax. We felt the Spanish combination of sensuality and dark moods, the flash of color and movement, sometimes slow, sometimes whirling, often fulfilling the promise of great beauty. The news Eduardo had just told us about Shambless's death added another dimension of danger to our performance.

We swirled onto the floor, one hand on a hip, the other arm held up, our fingers seducing the audience. We danced forward and back, always turning around and around, sometimes clapping, sometimes clicking our fingers. Our heads turned from side to side, then snapped back in an arrogant pose, our smiles tempting and provocative. We leaned backward, our heads up, our arms moving. We danced, now slowly, now faster and faster, flashing our legs through the slit in our skirts, building the excitement until the whole audience was leaning forward clapping with us, cheering us on. With a final burst of movement, we flung both arms in the air, and shouted, *"Olé!"*

The audience stood and yelled, *"Olé!"* with us, clapping and stamping their feet. We held hands and bowed, smiling, and said, "Thank you, *gracias,*" to our enthusiastic fans.

People surrounded us, shaking our hands, some hugging us, others saying, "That was sensational." Even the Spanish passengers complimented us. *"Excelente!"* They certainly had seen better flamenco dancing than ours, but they were nice enough to give us an A for effort. What we lacked in authenticity, we made up for in enthusiasm.

I tried not to think about what Eduardo told us, but it wasn't easy. I couldn't forget that I had wished Shambless dead just a short time ago. I wondered if he had died from all that wine and food that had obviously contributed to his obesity. Much as I disliked Shambless, I felt like we had been dancing on his grave.

We scurried behind a wide screen that had been set up at one end of the lounge car. We slid out of our tight, sequined dresses and dancing shoes into comfortable pants and blouses. My whole body said thank you. I know redheads aren't supposed to wear red, but I was in the mood for my burgundy blouse and black tights.

Somebody once told me you're supposed to wear red for courage. I had a feeling I would be needing a little courage in whatever was to follow Shambless's death. A few swipes of a comb and a quick shine of frosted watermelon lipstick turned me back into a woman ready for bear. The high that we got from dancing, especially flamenco stomping and clapping, did not go away when the music stopped. I was psyched. *What's next?* my hyped-up brain asked.

Tina, Janice, Pat, and Mary Louise were quick-change artists. They looked casual but sensational in long-sleeved silk blouses and tight black pants. We went back into the lounge car and headed toward the bar, stopping to talk to our enthusiastic fans along the way.

A tall, chic woman, her dark hair cut short and smooth, worked her way through the crowd surrounding us. She wore a form-fitting black dress with a turquoise necklace and earrings that made her eyes seem even bluer than they were.

"I'm Denise Morgan," she said. She held out her hand. "I hear you're from New Jersey—so am I. You guys are really good. I mean, I've seen a lot of dancers and you're terrific. You've got so much energy, you're so . . . sexy. Do you need an agent? I'd love to represent you."

"We've managed without one so far," Pat said, taking her hand. "But maybe it's time we had one. What do you think, guys? Should we hire this lady as our agent?"

"You really think we're good?" Tina asked.

"Yes, I do," Denise said. "I'm always looking for unusual acts, and five women in their . . ."

"In their prime of life," I said, finishing her sentence. I meant it. We looked good, had more energy than we'd had in years, felt alive and incredibly attractive.

Denise laughed. "Exactly," she said. "They wouldn't have hired you to entertain on this train if you weren't good. How long have you been doing this? Where else have you performed?"

"First Community Church in Chatham, New Jersey," I said. "The high school in Summit, New Jersey . . ."

"Come on, Gini," Tina said. "Cool it. Actually, Denise, we also danced on a cruise ship in Russia—the one that sails from Moscow to St. Petersburg—last year."

"I've been on that one," Denise said, "Tiny cabins, a German fräulein terrorizing her whole crew and passengers. The food was great, though."

"Sounds like you had a fun time," Pat said.

"It was . . . uh . . . interesting," Denise said. "Did you like it?"

"Well," Tina said, shuddering slightly, "The terrible British chef on our trip was fired. Tough for him, but great for us. A good Russian chef took over after him and we had excellent food. I mean, it was a fine cruise if you don't mind a couple of murders thrown in."

"What!" Denise said. "What do you mean 'a couple of murders'?"

"I mean, people were actually killed," I said. "Believe it or not, we helped solve the murders. I'd just as soon skip that experience this trip."

Then I remembered that Shambless was dead. What if we did have to go through that whole thing again on this journey? What if he didn't die from too much eating and drinking? What if he was murdered? I thought of Sylvia's look of hatred when she stopped at his table. She looked as if she wanted to kill him. A lot of people felt the same way. I tried to keep my face from showing the fear that overwhelmed me, but you know me. Everything shows.

"Are you all right, Gini?" Denise asked. "You look strange."

"I'm okay," I said. "It all came back to me for a minute."

"You kept dancing through murders and bad food?" Denise asked.

"That's us," I said. "The Happy Hoofers. We dance and solve murders at the same time." I tried to sound as if it were all one big adventure, but until I found out how Shambless had died, I was not exactly relaxed.

"I would love to represent you," Denise said. "If only to have a more interesting life."

"We'll talk some more," Pat said. "I'd love to hear more about your being our agent."

"Let's do that. You're . . . you're Pat, right?"

"Right. Talk to you later, Denise."

Pat watched her go as if she were an old friend. Denise joined another group of passengers nearby, but turned to catch a glimpse of Pat one more time. My friend had a far-away expression on her face.

"Pat?" I said.

"What? Why were you looking at me that way, Gini? What's the matter?"

"Nothing's the matter," I said. "It's just the look on your face—as if you knew her before. She knew your name, too, but not the rest of us."

"I know," Pat said. "Weird, isn't it? I feel like we were meant to meet on this train or she was the sister I never had or something."

"Knock it off, Shirley MacLaine," Janice said. "She's just an agent searching for clients. Maybe we should think about hiring someone, though."

"Mm-hmm," Pat said, looking over at Denise talking animatedly to another group of people. "Maybe we should."

The bar car was full of other passengers. The train could only hold fifty people, but when all of them were gathered in a narrow lounge car, it seemed like there were a lot more. We heard snatches of Spanish, German, French, and Norwegian as we wove our way through to the bar.

An unsmiling, stocky man somewhere in his forties was making martinis and cosmos for the Americans, pouring beer for the Germans, serving *cava* to the Spanish, and wine to the French travelers. I heard someone call him Juan. Nothing seemed to rattle him, no matter what people ordered. I asked him for a *cava*.

"You're American and you're not having a cosmo or a margarita?" he said.

"Is that all Americans drink now?" Mary Louise asked.

"Ever since that show—you know, that TV show—with those women—making love in the city or something—that's all they order."

"I still want a *cava*," I said.

"Good choice, señora," Juan said.

Lined up along one end of the bar were trays full of delicious-looking little hors d'oeuvres. My first bite of something crusty and spicy made me ask Juan, "Mmm, what is this? It's fantastic."

Juan didn't smile. I wasn't sure if he ever smiled. "Those are called *tigres*, señora."

"I'm eating little tigers?" I asked, trying to get him to laugh a little.

"Not tigers," he said. "Mussels. Mussels stuffed with onion, pepper, tomato sauce, then breaded and fried."

"They're incredible," I said. "Mary Louise, you have to try one of these."

She bit into one of the *tigres* and closed her eyes in ecstasy.

"These are heavenly," she said, taking another one. "Juan, do you think I could get the recipe for these? My husband would love them."

"I will ask, señora," Juan said. There was a hint of a smile on his face at her enthusiastic reaction to the tapas. He continued, uncharacteristically garrulous, "You might like to join the chef for a cooking class on tapas. He'll show you how to make these *tigres* and several other tapas."

"Absolutely," Mary Louise said. "When is he doing that?"

"Probably tomorrow. They will announce it."

"If he makes these deviled eggs with shrimp, I want to come too," Janice said. "And these too—red peppers with anchovies. They're fantastic."

"You'd think we hadn't eaten for days," Pat said, reaching for a ham croquette. "But these are the best hors d'oeuvres—I guess I should call them tapas."

I squeezed in next to two women, the older one drinking a glass of wine, the younger a cosmo.

"How's the wine?" I asked.

When the older woman turned to answer me, I recognized her from our encounter at the restaurant. The one with the French accent who had told me not to get upset by Shambless's rudeness. She was stunning. Dark-haired. Beautiful complexion. High cheekbones. She wore a white lacy dress that clung to her figure, and delicate pearl drop earrings that were perfect with the dress. I don't know what it is exactly, but many French women have a certain look that says, "I am my own woman. Don't mess with me."

"It's not bad," she said. "Not quite as dry as I like, but it's fine."

I'm a Francophile because of the year I spent studying photography in Paris, so I had to ask. "Are you French?"

"I am," she said, holding out her hand. "I'm Danielle, and this is my daughter, Michele."

Michele was in her twenties, blonde, very pretty with hardly any makeup on her smooth skin. She wore a lavender silky blouse with white pants. She had her mother's warm personality.

"I loved watching you dance," she said. "You put your whole heart and soul into your performance. I love dancing, too, but don't get much of a chance to do it."

"Michele cofounded a company that finances start-up computer companies. They specialize in wearable technology. I have no idea what that is, but she seems to love it."

Michele's laugh was musical and delightful to listen to. She didn't have a trace of a French accent, but there was something else in there that I couldn't detect at first.

"Your English is perfect," I said to her. "Where did you learn it?"

Danielle interrupted. "I'm married to an Englishman," she said. "We live in England, but my husband spends a lot of time in France. That's how we met. I was working at the UN as a translator. I acted as an interpreter for him when his work took him to Paris. After a while, he decided he couldn't do without me and whisked me off to England. Michele grew up in England, but she lives in San Francisco now."

"Did your husband come with you on this trip?" Mary Louise asked.

"Yes, but as usual he's on the phone," Michele said.

Danielle frowned at her daughter.

"My husband works very hard," she said. "Sometimes it's hard for Michele to understand that he loves what he does and it takes up a lot of his time."

"What does he do?" I asked

"He's a barrister," she said.

"My husband's a lawyer too," Mary Louise said.

"Really?" Danielle said, looking at Mary Louise with interest. "Is he with you on this trip?"

"No, he's home," Mary Louise said. "Like your husband, he's always working. I guess it's an occupational hazard with lawyers. They never get time off." Then her face brightened and she clicked her fingers together, flamenco style.

"Olé," she said. "I miss him, but I love dancing on this ship."

"I can see why," Danielle said. "You were—oh, what is the word I'm looking for, Michele—you were formidable." She pronounced it the French way: *for-mee-dah-bleu.*

"Formidable is right, Mom," Michele said, pronouncing it the English way. "Unbeatable. I always wanted to be a dancer, too, but my father convinced me to follow a more serious career. Every once in a while, though, I sneak off and dance. He also thinks I should marry somebody in the royal family."

"I think there's only one eligible royal left," I said. "That cute Harry is still available."

Michele laughed. "Hey, I'd give up my career to marry him any day."

"I hope you're not being irreverent about the royal family," a man with a British accent said, coming up and hugging Michele and kissing Danielle. He was stunningly British, tall and polished, with lots of wavy dark hair, and good teeth.

"Hello, darling," Danielle said. "Meet Mary Louise and Gini."

"You were brilliant back there," he said, pronouncing it *breeyant.* "I'm Geoffrey." He held out his hand.

"I thought you never left your phone," I said.

"You've been talking to my daughter," he said, kissing her on the cheek. "She thinks all I do is work."

"Well, it's true," Michele said. "But I love you anyway."

"I'm glad of that," Geoffrey said, smiling at his daughter. "What would you ladies like to drink?"

Pat spoke first. "Just a lemonade for me, please."

Thud. I felt all the excitement dribbling onto the floor. Lemonade. After all that stamping and clapping and whirling and flirting. After all that seduction and lust in the air while we danced, I wanted champagne, or at least *cava,* which is the Spanish version of champagne. Bubbles and fun and the feeling that anything could happen.

Come to think of it, what I really wanted was Alex Boyer, my Alex, whom I met on our cruise in Russia, where he was bureau chief of *The New York Times* in Moscow. He's an adventure junkie like me. We fell in love on that trip. Alex left the Moscow Bureau to return to *The Times* office in New York to be near me. I missed him. I'd give him a call later on when our time zones meshed. Six hours' difference made it difficult to keep up with each other.

My friends seemed to have squashed their desire for a drink out of consideration for Pat. That was certainly the least I could do for our pal, who was trying her best to resist the urge for alcohol. I didn't really want lemonade, though. That would be too boring.

"Never mind the *cava,* Juan. I'll have a ginger ale, please," I said. At least it would be bubbly.

The others ordered soft drinks or coffee.

Pat saw the look on my face. I tried to stay expressionless, but it was no use. She knew exactly what I was thinking.

"You don't have to do this for me," Pat said to us. "I'm fine. If I can't go without alcohol in a place filled with people drinking, I haven't really beaten it. Please, you guys, go ahead and order what you want. I won't suddenly lapse into a crazed yearning for a drink."

"We know you won't," Mary Louise said. "You're a lot stronger than the rest of us. But we don't really need a drink. We're still high on that music, the excitement of flamenco. The way the audience reacted. Sometimes I think I'm only truly alive when I'm dancing. I change somehow. I don't know, I'm more than myself. I have . . ."

"You have duende," a friendly-looking, shaggy-haired man said, approaching us to stand next to her. He was tall and casually dressed in jeans and a blue shirt with rolled-up sleeves. He had the kind of face and manner that you trusted immediately. Some people are like that. It's the direct way they look you in the eye or a mouth that looks ready to smile.

"You were incredible out there on that floor," he said. "Hello, I'm Mike Parnell."

"Mike's an old friend of ours from the days when we lived in New York," Geoffrey said. "I persuaded him to come on this trip with us."

"Hi, Mike," I said. "Are you a lawyer too?"

"Not a chance!" he said. "I'm an obstetrician—I delivered Michele."

He could not keep his eyes off of Mary Louise. "Forgive me for staring," he said. "But you look so familiar. Have we met?"

"I don't think so," she said. "I had all my babies in New Jersey. Do you ever come to New Jersey?"

"Not if I can help it," he said, the laugh lines around his eyes crinkling. "I'm kidding. I'm sure New Jersey is a very nice place. Snooki seems to like it."

Mary Louise laughed. She was clearly attracted to this warm, friendly man. "You could have delivered her baby if you had deigned to come there. It's the Garden State of America, you know."

"Must be a rock garden," he said, causing me to choke on my ginger ale. "I once saw a clip from some show called *Real Housewives of New Jersey*. They were throwing drinks at each other and knocking tables over. I just assumed that all women in New Jersey were like that."

"You have a lot to learn about my state," Mary Louise said. "We only throw drinks at people if they say bad things about us."

"I can see I have a lot to learn," he said, putting his hand gently on Mary Louise's shoulder. Will you teach me?"

Her smile faded. She was looking at the wedding ring on his left hand. "Is your wife with you on this trip?" she asked.

He hesitated, "No, she . . ."

"Jenny died two years ago," Danielle said, putting her arm around Mike.

"Oh, Mike, I'm so sorry," Mary Louise said.

"Thank you," he said. "I still find it hard to talk about her because I miss her so much. You know, you look like her, Mary Louise. Maybe that's why I thought I'd seen you before. She had the same lovely skin, the same blue eyes you—" he stopped, looking at her left hand. "Is your husband with you on this trip?"

She touched her ring. "No, he's in the middle of a trial. I think it's a relief for him when I go on these trips."

"I would think he'd want to be with you all the time. Where does he practice?"

"In New York. The commute is a killer, but we wanted to bring our children up in the suburbs."

"How many children do you have?" Mike asked. It was as if he didn't want to let her go, as if he wanted to find out everything he could about her.

"Three—two boys and a girl. My two oldest are in college and the youngest, my daughter, is a senior in high school. How about you?"

"Twin daughters," he said. "They're both seniors in high school too."

"Do you live in the city?"

"Yes, that's where my patients are. I have to admit, I love being in New York. There's so much going on all the time. You never know what's going to happen next in that crazy city."

"It must be wonderful spending your days bringing new life into the world," Mary Louise said.

His whole face lit up. "You have no idea," he said. "Every baby is a little miracle to me. I know that sounds trite, but even when it's a difficult birth, the feeling of adding a new being to the world is always incredibly rewarding. You'd think I'd be over that by now. I've been doing it such a long time, but it's still wonderful." He looked embarrassed, as if he had said more than he meant to, expressed more emotion that he wanted to.

"All doctors should feel like that," Mary Louise said softly.

They were silent. I saw the rapt look in Mary Louise's eyes as she listened to this man. I couldn't blame her. He was the kind of man you wanted to wrap up and take home with you.

"But you didn't tell me," Mary Louise said. "What's duende?"

"It's hard to describe," Mike said. "It's a kind of charisma, a sort of force that takes over a performer when she becomes part of the music. I asked a flamenco guitar player about it once. He said it's when you rise above yourself to become something more than you are ordinarily. I don't know if I'm saying this right, but you always know when you've achieved it. The audience knows too. You and your friends did it tonight up there on that stage."

He called to Eduardo, who was talking to some people near us.

"Eduardo," he said. "Am I right? Don't you think these beautiful women had duende when they did that flamenco? Have I used the word correctly?"

Eduardo hesitated. "Well, they certainly came close," he said. "But, forgive me please, ladies, the flamenco is so uncompromisingly Spanish. Not even northern Spanish, but southern Spanish. It's part of the soul of Andalusia. Or actually the soul of gypsies. You did come close. You were very good. But to feel the real duende, you have to see the flamenco sung and danced by gypsies. Especially sung. It's unique. Deeply felt. Sort of a wailing, an ecstasy, a . . . You have to be there."

When I heard Eduardo describe this magic that happens when you know you've achieved something exquisitely unique, something you didn't know you could do, I understood why I love to dance. It doesn't happen very often, but when it does it's immensely moving. It's as if my body takes over from my mind. I stop thinking and let the music take over.

Sometimes it happens when I'm filming too. I capture a moment. Not just a scene or a person's face, but a moment in time that says something important about life. It happened when I was filming the firemen on 9/11. One man came out carrying a young woman who was killed when the plane crashed into her office. There were tears running down his face, making a path on his blackened cheeks. When I took his picture, I cried, too. That photograph captured the grief of that day when so many people died for no reason. Young and old, they were victims of a hatred they had done nothing to cause.

"Well, at least we came close," Mary Louise said.

"Very close," Michele said. "Your passion was tangible. It was wonderful to watch."

I envied this bright, lovely girl her youth. I usually don't want to be any younger than I am right now, but I saw her smooth skin, her interest in everything going on around her, and I wished—just for a second—to be in my twenties again. I remembered feeling that there was nothing I couldn't do. Each age has its magic moments. Her whole life was ahead of her.

Mike started to say something to Mary Louise when Eduardo pulled him aside. He whispered something in Mike's ear that obviously surprised him. I knew it had to be about Shambless. I was dying to find out what was going on. How could it still be a big secret? Why weren't the police there? Obviously, Mike knew something we didn't know, or Eduardo wouldn't be consulting him.

"Excuse me, Eduardo needs my help. I have to go," Mike said. He obviously didn't want to leave Mary Louise. "To be continued, Jersey girl," he said.

Eduardo grabbed his arm and pulled Mike from the room.

Mary Louise watched him go. I knew exactly what was going through her mind. She saw the look on my face. "Don't say it, Gini," she said.

You know me. I can never not say what I'm thinking. "He likes you, Mary Louise," I said.

"I know. And I . . . I can't help it, Gini. I like him too."

"It's written all over your face," I said, more sharply than I meant to. "You're married—remember? You've got all those children. And he's really vulnerable. You remind him of his wife."

"Come on, Gini," Mary Louise said. "I never do anything I'm not supposed to do. I'm plain old boring, married me, faithful to plain old boring, married George."

Mary Louise is so nice we have to yell at her to get her to stand up for herself.

"You've never been boring a day in your life," I said. I didn't yell, but I was firm.

"Oh, look," she said. "Janice is over there at that table by the window talking to Tom. I didn't see her before. Let's go join them."

"I'm not sure they want to be interrupted," I said.

"I see what you mean. They're totally into each other."

Janice and Tom were talking intently. They might as well have been alone. They seemed unaware of other people walking by their table. Tom reached over and touched her face gently. She covered his hand with her own. He looked as if he were about to kiss her when Sylvia walked up behind him. Her voice was low and angry but loud enough for Mary Louise and me to hear.

"Don't let me interrupt anything," she said. Everything about Sylvia was gray. Her hair, her complexion, her blouse and skirt, her sandals. She didn't wear any makeup. There were deep frown lines between her eyebrows. I wondered if she ever smiled.

"Sylvia," Tom said. "Where did you go after we got back from the restaurant? I looked for you everywhere."

"Doesn't seem like you looked too hard," she said. "When did you set this little meeting up?"

"He didn't set anything up, Sylvia," Janice said. "We just walked into this car at the same time and started to talk, to catch up." She stood up and pushed back her chair. "I'm tired. Think I'll head for bed. Nothing happened, Sylvia. Really." And she hurried out of the bar car, her face miserable.

"Why don't you follow her?" Sylvia said to

Tom, her voice getting louder, angrier. "If you want to be with that woman, go ahead. You seem to prefer her over me."

People near them moved away, uncomfortable at Sylvia's anger. Mary Louise and I stayed where we were, but it was impossible not to hear them.

"Janice and I are old friends, Sylvia," Tom said. He looked weary, sick of this whole scene. "I like talking to her. That's all there is to it. Let it go."

But Sylvia wouldn't stop. She leaned closer to him, her face twisted and belligerent. "You looked like more than friends to me."

"Think what you want," Tom said, his voice low and resentful. "You always do. I don't want to listen to any more of this." He walked away from her and out of the car.

Sylvia lit a cigarette and noticed us standing nearby.

"Tell your friend to stay away from him," she said. "I mean it."

"Relax, Sylvia," I said. "Janice isn't after Tom."

"She's not like that," Mary Louise said.

"She didn't look so harmless to me," Sylvia said. "I'm not a fool. I can tell when somebody is after my husband. I know they were in that play together. She was in love with him then. He's lucky he didn't marry her. I hear she's been divorced three times. She probably would have dumped him too. Just tell her to watch it." She turned and walked over to the bar and ordered a margarita.

Mary Louise pulled me away before I could say anything more. "Forget it, Gini. Let her alone. Let's go see if Janice is okay," she said. We left the bar car.

"That woman is angry all the time," Mary Louise said as we walked down the corridor.

"Seems like it," I said. "Poor Tom. Too bad he didn't marry Janice."

"He might have been her third divorce. Jan always says she was a mess back then."

We knocked on her door and found Janice staring out the window, a crumpled tissue in her hand. There were tears in her eyes when she turned to greet us.

"Are you okay?" Mary Louise asked.

"Not really. I feel sorry for Tom," Jan said.

"Me too," I said. "She's a witch. And she's really convinced that you'll take Tom away from her. If you ask me, Tom's had enough. You should rescue him."

"You know me better than that, Gini. I would never do anything to encourage Tom. He's a wonderful guy, but he's married to Sylvia. I don't know why, but he is. He loved her enough to marry her. That's it."

"Too bad," I said. "You two would make a great couple."

"Troublemaker," Janice said, trying not to smile.

I said good night to my friends and went back

to the suite I shared with Tina. The room was small. After all, it was a narrow-gauge railroad, but both Tina and I are on the petite side. I'm five feet three and weigh 108 on good days. She's five feet four and is around 110. Our weight varies according to how much pastry we have for breakfast, how much starch and sugar we cram in the rest of the day, and how strenuous our dance is. After the flamenco I was feeling absolutely svelte.

There were two single beds in our suite, a fairly big closet, a comfortable couch that seated one and a half thin people, a table to write or eat on, and a small but adequate bathroom with a shower, sink, and toilet.

Tina is the travel editor at *Perfect Bride* magazine and recommends honeymoon trips to her readers. When we first dumped our stuff in this small room, I asked her, "Tina, think this is big enough for your newlyweds?"

"They don't need a lot of room," she said. "They're not going to do much in here except rumple the sheets. They get a double bed."

Our three friends were crammed into a slightly larger suite next door with a bunk bed for the smallest one.

"How come I get to room with you and not squashed into the room next door with two other hoofers?" I asked.

"Because you would have complained the whole trip," Tina said.

"I know I can be a royal pain in the ass sometimes," I said.

"Sometimes!" Tina said. "How about all the time? But we love you anyway."

"Thanks for choosing me to be your roommate, Tina. I hope our friends aren't too smashed together next door."

"They'll manage," Tina said. "It's only for a week, after all."

It was one in the morning and I was tired. The high from the dancing was gone. I just wanted to climb into my twin bed and sleep until my body said, "Wake up."

Tina was asleep before I finished brushing my teeth.

Chapter 3

Murder, He Said

The next morning we had just finished dress-ing when we heard people running up and down the corridor. I pulled myself up and peered out the window. There was an ambulance outside the train. Men and women in white coats were boarding.

I opened the door of our suite as Carlos ran past.

"What's going on, Carlos?" I asked him.

"There has been an . . . an incident."

"You mean Shambless's death," I said. "Did they find out what he died of?"

"I don't know, señora. I have to go. Excuse me."

Mary Louise stuck her head out of her suite.

"What's up, Gini?" she asked.

"I'm not sure," I told her. "Did you see the ambulance out there? Must be for Shambless. "

"Yes, I saw it before. There were too many people to see what was happening."

I went into her suite. We looked out her window again over Janice's and Pat's heads. As we watched, we saw Mike Parnell leave the group near the ambulance and get back on the train.

Mary Louise stopped him as he walked past our suite. "Mike, what's the matter? What's happening out there?"

"Oh, Mary Louise—hello. That talk show guy—Shambless. I'm afraid he's dead."

"I know. Eduardo told us about it before we danced last night. But he wouldn't tell us what happened. Do you know what he died of? Are you the doctor they called when they found him?"

"Yeah," Mike said. "They won't know what caused his death until after the medical examiner's report. Carlos found him. He ran to tell Eduardo, who called me because I'm the only doctor on the train. There's no way of telling what he died of until they finish their tests. He could have had a heart attack. Or he could have passed out from drinking a whole bottle of wine at dinner last night, then choked to death. He could have died from food poisoning. They didn't really give me a chance to examine him. "

"So, now what?" I asked him.

"We wait until the police come. The police can't move the body until they have a chance to make a thorough examination of the room in case his death was caused by foul play. I'm sure they won't let anybody off the train until they're through, so we probably won't get to Ribadeo today."

"I was looking forward to that," I said. "Eduardo told me I would get some really beautiful shots there."

"He's right, Gini. It is incredible," Mike said. "I've been there. It's the perfect Galician town. You'll get some great photographs when we finally get there. I'm sure we'll see it soon, but we won't be going anywhere until the police talk to us."

"What's going on?" Michele asked, running up to us. "How come there's an ambulance out there?

"Shambless died last night, Michele," I told her. "Carlos found his body. Nobody knows what caused his death yet."

"He was a terrible man," she said. "A lot of people will be glad he's gone."

Eduardo, his face drawn and agonized, got back on the train.

"What's happening?" Tina asked him.

"I can't really talk about it," Eduardo said. Then, being Eduardo, always the polite host, he said, "Breakfast will be a little late. I'm so sorry."

"What killed him?" I asked.

"Well, I'm not sure," Eduardo said, his innate discretion warring with his desire to tell us what he knew. "That is . . . well, the police have asked us not to say anything."

"Do we have to stay in our suites or is it okay to go into the dining car?" I asked.

"I think it's all right for you to go. I don't know why not. I just . . . Please excuse me. I have to talk to the police. I'll let you know as soon as I find out something." He walked quickly down the corridor into the next car.

We exchanged glances. Coffee. Now. We headed for the dining car. Along the way, other passengers poked their heads out of their suites and asked us what was going on. Had we heard anything? Was someone ill? What about breakfast?

We told them we had no idea. We said we were going for coffee and would try to find out more.

By the time we got to the dining car, several passengers had already arrived, looking confused and asking questions in Spanish, German, English, and Norwegian.

The dining car was long and narrow with tables for two on each side of an aisle. A buffet table beckoned from the far end. I took a quick peek and saw only the large urns containing coffee and hot water for tea. There was no food to be seen.

We got our beverages and sat down. The wood in the dining room was dark and polished. The sconces held exquisite lamps that looked like they had been there since the 1890s. Everything was elegant, classic, perfect. I wanted to photograph every inch of this car. I imagined this is what the dining car on the Orient Express must have looked like. Not that I'd ever get a chance to ride on such an incredibly expensive train—unless, of course, they hired us to dance on it. Now there's an idea.

"Hey, Tina," I said. "Think you could get us a gig dancing on the Orient Express?"

"Dream on, Gini," she said.

Tom edged his way into the car and stopped at our table. "Hi, hoofers, what's going on? I can't get anyone to tell me anything. I came back here to get breakfast. They said they weren't sure when it would be ready and would I like some coffee while I wait."

He was really talking to one person in our group. We all knew it.

"Are you okay, Jan?" he asked, his face showing his concern.

"Sort of," she said. "That talk show guy—you know, the loud, obnoxious blabbermouth, the one who fired Sylvia—is dead. Nobody knows what he died of. They're going to take him to the lab for tests."

"Wait till Sylvia hears this!" Tom said.

"Where is she?" Janice asked. "Why isn't she with you?"

"She's coming," Tom said. "She was still getting dressed when I left. She was up late last night. She said she couldn't sleep and was going to watch TV in the lounge car."

The door of the dining car opened and a quintessentially Spanish man, dark hair, gray at the temples, lined face, serious expression, aquiline nose, dark brown, almost black eyes, walked in and strode to the front of the car in front of the buffet table. Everyone stopped talking.

"Good morning, señores and señoras. I'm Inspector Javier Cruz," he said. "There was a death on this train last night. The medical examiner has established that Señor Shambless was poisoned. I would like to ask each of you a few questions. I would appreciate it if you would move into the lounge car where there is more room. You can bring your coffee with you. I hope we do not have to inconvenience you for very long."

"He's gorgeous," Janice whispered to me.

"There's something about Spanish men that's—different, sort of intense," I whispered back. "I don't know what it is, but it's very sexy."

"Can I have him?" Janice said.

"He's all yours," I said. I love watching Janice entice a man into her web. She just sort of stands there, looking unattainable and beautiful. There isn't a man I've ever seen who can resist her. She's also the least organized of any of us. We have to keep making lists for her so she'll bring what she needs for the costumes we wear for our dances. We stick Post-its all over her purse and text her all the time so she won't forget anything.

I'm sure most men wouldn't care if she forgot her name as long as they could look at her.

We inched our way into the lounge car, where we all crowded together to wait for the inspector's questions.

He took Mike aside first. I moved closer so I could hear their conversation. Holding up the local newspaper, *Noticias del Dia,* I pretended to be fascinated by the coverage of a soccer match. The action photos of the game were actually quite well done.

"What did Shambless look like when you saw him last night, Dr. Parnell?"

"He was a mess, Inspector. There was vomit and feces all over the bed. He had tried to reach for the bell to call someone, but his bulk kept him from turning over. He was half in the bed and half out of it. I assumed he drank too much and choked on his own vomit. I didn't really have a chance to examine him thoroughly, though."

"What did you do?"

"I told Eduardo to call the police squad right away and then I left. I stayed until the medical examiner came."

"Did it occur to you that he might have been poisoned?"

"No, I just thought it could have been flu or

some kind of gastrointestinal upset. Poison didn't occur to me. I couldn't really examine him because the medical crew was on its way. I had to leave."

"Do you have any idea who could have killed him?"

"No," Mike said. "It could have been anybody on the train or in the restaurant. He made a lot of people angry because he was so rude. I leave it up to you to find his killer, Inspector."

"Thank you, Doctor. If you think of anything that might be helpful, let me know."

"Of course."

The inspector walked over to the blonde huddled in the corner with Steve, the photographer. With her face free of makeup, she seemed younger, more vulnerable than she did the night before. She looked defiant when the inspector approached her. I turned the page of my newspaper and edged closer to hear her answers.

"You were traveling with Señor Shambless?" he asked her.

She nodded. "I was," she said.

"I understand he was making a documentary of this trip. Were you helping him or . . . what exactly were you doing, Miss . . . ?"

She sat up straight. "Callahan. Julie Callahan. I was directing the documentary," she said.

The inspector glanced up at the photographer in time to catch a small smile on his face when Julie said that. He spoke to him.

"And you are . . . ?"

"Steve Bergman, Inspector. I'm the camera guy for this trip."

He looked like a lot of the men I've seen when I've been covering a story. Shaggy-haired, a little paunchy from too much beer, eyes darting around to get the right angle for a photo, somewhere in his thirties.

"How well did you know Señor Shambless before this trip?" the inspector asked.

"He wasn't like a buddy," Steve said. "I've done some publicity shots for him, but this is the first time I've done a documentary for him."

"Do either of you have any idea why someone would want to kill Mr. Shambless?"

They exchanged glances and didn't answer at first.

Finally, Julie said in a voice so low I could barely hear her, "Of course not. Everyone loved him."

"Yeah, loved him," Steve said.

"You don't sound very convincing, Señor Bergman," Inspector Cruz said. "Do you have reason to believe that someone did not love him? Perhaps wanted to kill him?"

"Inspector, besides the millions of people who did love him, there were just as many who didn't," Steve said. "He told me he got threats all the time. He usually traveled with a bodyguard, but I guess this time he thought he wouldn't need one because I was here to protect him."

"I thought he was a popular talk show host in your country," Cruz said.

"Oh, he got top ratings. There are a lot of people who think he was the greatest thing since sliced bread. And a lot who wished he would shut up and get off of TV."

"How about you, Señor Bergman? Did you like him?"

"I wasn't crazy about him. I'm no right-wing nut. But this was a good gig. All I had to do was take pictures of this part of Spain. Green Spain, I think they call it. Right? It's beautiful here. The mountains, the ocean, the white houses. I had to keep reminding myself to take pictures of him."

The inspector nodded in agreement. "This is my favorite part of our country," he said. "Even with all the rain. That's why it's Green Spain."

He addressed Julie again. "Did you share his suite with him?" he asked.

She flashed him a hostile glance. I didn't think she was going to answer. But lifting her chin, she said, "No, he likes to be alone. I had my own room."

The inspector looked at some notes on his iPad. "Some people in the restaurant last night got the impression that you were quarreling with him. They said you asked him about doing something and Shambless said it would have to wait. Then, they said, you got up and left the table and waited for him outside the restaurant. They seemed to think that perhaps your relationship was more personal than just director of the documentary. Is that true?"

She shifted in her seat, looked at Steve, and then said, "I don't know whom you were talking to. It was nothing personal, nothing serious at all. He complained about the food at the restaurant. I told him this part of Spain is famous for its seafood, and he should at least try it. You know, for the sake of the documentary. But he insisted on ordering a steak and French fries."

The inspector's expression was skeptical. He raised one eyebrow and continued. "I understand from some people at the next table that you wanted him to do something he didn't want to do. He got annoyed with you for bringing it up. Is that correct?"

"We disagreed on what to put in the documentary, that's all," Julie said. "I thought we should have more scenes outside. He wanted more pictures of himself eating and talking to his devoted fans. He didn't seem to notice that he didn't have too many fans on this train. Just that idiot woman who asked for his autograph."

"Which 'idiot woman' are you talking about?"

"I don't know her name. She's always talking about what a great man he is."

"Is she here in this room now?"

Julie looked around. "I don't see her."

Dora, who had been standing near the bar,

hidden behind some taller people, stepped forward.

"If you're trying to find the 'idiot woman' who thinks Shambless was a great man, I guess that's me," she said. She looked at Julie. "You have some nerve calling me an idiot. You're the one he was trying to get rid of."

"I apologize for the use of that term," Javier said. "Please stay here, señora. I would like to ask you some questions in a few minutes."

"I'd be glad to answer any questions you might have to find the evil person who killed one of our country's most revered men," she said.

The inspector turned back to Julie.

"That's all you disagreed about? What should or should not go into the documentary?"

"Yes, that's it. Can I go now?"

The inspector took some rapid notes, and then said, "You may go, but we'll talk about this again later."

Julie stood up and walked quickly out of the car. People moved aside to let her through. The lounge car was barely big enough to hold all the passengers. Some of the younger people were sitting on the floor.

I edged a little closer to the inspector to hear better as he started to question Steve. I tried to be as inconspicuous as possible, just another tourist wrapped up in the local newspaper. I could hear every word.

"Any idea what they quarreled about?" the inspector asked Steve. "Was it the documentary?"

Steve looked away from the inspector. He was obviously uncomfortable.

"Señor Bergman?" the inspector said.

"Listen, Inspector, I don't want to say anything to get her in trouble. She's a good kid."

"I understand your loyalty, but it would help me if you could tell me what the problem was."

Steve took a deep breath. "Well, see," he said, "it wasn't about the documentary. She didn't really have much to do with that."

"I thought she was directing the film," the inspector said.

Steve shook his head. "Not really," he said. "That's what Shambless told people, but she was really here to . . . uh . . . to keep him company. As a . . . uh . . . companion."

"You mean they were lovers?" the inspector said. "Is that what you mean by 'to keep him company'?"

"I guess you could say that," Steve mumbled, cracking his knuckles, clearly uneasy talking about this.

The inspector persisted. "What was the quarrel about?"

Steve put his head in his hands, his hair flopping in his eyes. I could hardly hear his words when he continued, so I got a little closer. The inspector looked up and frowned at me, so I moved back an inch.

"She thought he was going to marry her," Steve said. "Look, he was a rat—okay? He lied to her. She believed him when he said he was going to divorce his wife. Then, on this trip, he kept putting her off. It was obvious—well, it was obvious to me anyhow—that he had no intention of marrying her. He was just lying to her. I felt sorry for her. Like I said, she's a good kid."

"Did you see her last night after returning from the restaurant?"

"Just for a minute. I went into the bar to get a drink. Shambless was already there and Julie was trying to talk to him. I heard her ask him if he felt all right, if he needed anything, but he pushed her away. I heard him tell her to leave him alone. She got into a conversation with the bartender after that, but I couldn't hear what they were talking about. I assumed she had a drink and went back to her suite."

"Thank you, Señor Bergman," the inspector said. "You've been very helpful."

The inspector began to question another passenger but turned around to say something else to Steve.

"Señor Bergman, *por favor.* One more question. Did you film the restaurant and Señor Shambless for the documentary last night?"

"I did."

"Mostly in the restaurant or outside?"

"Both, Inspector."

"I assume you also have footage of Shambless himself?"

"Some—not a lot. I wanted to get him with his fans, but there was only that one woman who asked for his autograph. The one Julie mentioned. I got some shots of her with Shambless."

"Would you be kind enough to show me what you filmed?"

"Sure, Inspector. I'll get my camera. I left it on the table in the dining room."

"Thank you," the inspector said. He turned to talk to the person standing nearest to him, Shamblesss's devoted fan, Dora. I pretended to point out a newspaper article to Mary Louise, but I was really listening to the inspector's questions and Dora's answers.

"You were a big fan of Señor Shambless, I understand," he said.

"Yes," she said, twisting her hands together. "I must say I resent being called an idiot by that blond tramp. He was a wonderful man, Inspector. Just wonderful." She pressed her fingers against her forehead. "Would you mind if I talked to you later? I just realized I need something in my cabin. A pill. I'm getting one of my really bad headaches."

"Of course, señora. Come back when you're feeling better. Again, I apologize for the use of the word *idiot*."

Dora scurried out of the car. The inspector walked around the packed car, asking several people a few questions, listening intently to their answers, moving from group to group until he got to the five of us.

He addressed me first. "I hope I spoke loudly enough for you to hear my questions to the other passengers, Señora Miller." His smile was sardonic. I have to admit I was a little embarrassed. But I certainly wasn't going to let him know that.

"I don't know what you mean, Inspector," I said. "This car is really crowded. I couldn't help being close to you at times. I'm sorry if you thought I was eavesdropping." I didn't sound convincing even to myself. The inspector let it go.

"You produce documentaries, Señora Miller, no?" he asked.

"I produce documentaries, yes," I said.

"What kind of films have you done?"

"I did one on Hurricane Katrina in New Orleans. One on 9/11. One on an orphanage in India."

"Are you filming a documentary on this train trip?"

"No, I'm just an entertainer on this ride," I said. "But there is certainly a lot to photograph in your beautiful country. I was hoping we'd get to Ribadeo today because I hear it's a filmmaker's dream. Any chance we'll be able to leave the train?"

The inspector smiled at me. Maybe he's not so bad after all, I thought. "It is indeed a beautiful country," he said, his tone a little friendlier.

"Especially Ribadeo. I'm not sure if you will be able to see it today, though, señora. It depends on how much information I can gather from you and your fellow passengers."

"Ask me anything you want, Inspector. I have no secrets."

He consulted his notes. His expression changed. He didn't look all that friendly anymore. "I understand you said you'd like to kill Señor Shambless on the bus last night," he said.

I stared at him, stunned. We seemed to be having a nice, civilized conversation about my work and Spain. Then wham! He hit me with this. I started to speak. At first nothing came out of my mouth. For the billionth time in my life, I wished that I didn't always say the first thing that popped into my mind.

"I might have," I said, my voice rising with each word. "I certainly didn't like him. He was an obnoxious fool. But who told you I said that?"

"One of the other passengers heard you. Several other people heard you quarreling with him in the restaurant and then threatening to kill him on the bus. Why didn't you like him?"

Uh-oh, this was starting to get serious, I thought. I tried to talk more calmly, but it was no use. I'm just not a calm person when I feel threatened. Maybe you've noticed.

"Because he spewed hatred and narrow-mindedness on television every day," I said, my voice getting louder. "I think he's responsible for a lot of bullying that goes on in this world."

The inspector leaned closer to me. He lowered his voice. He sounded like a prosecutor. "What kind of bullying?"

"Especially toward gay people," I said, trying to return this whole interrogation into a reasonable conversation. "He was always ranting against gay marriage and gay people. And he hated strong women. He wished we'd all shut up and cook."

The inspector paused. "Do you consider yourself a strong woman, Señora Miller?"

"Yes, I do," I said. "Does that bother you, Inspector?" I know, I know. Not a good answer. Sue me.

"Sometimes a strong woman can be . . . overwhelming."

"Inspector Cruz," I said. "Just because I'm strong doesn't mean that I go around killing people who disagree with me. There would be dead bodies all over the place if I did that." I was trying to get him to lighten up, but it didn't work. He changed the subject.

"Where were you after you got back from the restaurant?" he asked.

"My friends and I performed for the other passengers."

"What exactly did you perform?" the inspector asked. I resented his tone. What did he think we were—pole dancers?

"We're the Happy Hoofers," I said. I could see from the look on his face he had no idea what that meant.

"Dancers, Inspector. We were hired to dance on this train."

"What kind of dance did you do?"

"The flamenco," I said. I clicked my fingers, stamped my heels, and said, *"Olé!"* Not even the beginning of a smile.

"You did a Spanish dance?" he asked. I can only describe the expression on his face as a sneer.

"Yes, the flamenco," I said. "We thought it would be the best way to introduce ourselves to the other passengers, many of whom are Spanish, by doing that. It was our attempt to honor their country. Your country."

"Admirable," the inspector said without meaning it. I knew what he really meant. Americans have no right to muck up one of the finest traditions of Spanish culture.

"What did you do after you, um, danced?" he asked.

"We hung around talking to people. Do you suspect me of anything, Inspector?" I asked, really annoyed at this man.

"I'm just trying to get some information. Do you always take offense when people ask you questions?"

I was about to explode and say things I shouldn't when Tina moved closer to me and put a gentling hand on my arm.

"Inspector," she said in her most charming voice. Believe me, nobody is more charming than Tina when she puts her mind to it. "Gini has a short fuse, but she's not a murderer. She was with us all the time after we got back from the restaurant. She and I share a suite. She certainly didn't get up in the middle of the night and kill anyone. I would have noticed."

"You share a suite?" he asked.

"Yes, the suite we were assigned by Eduardo," Tina said.

"You have a problem with that?" I asked, noticing the raised eyebrow on his face again.

"No, no, señora," he said. "No problem at all. Thank you for your cooperation." He didn't look all that grateful. "Please be available for more questions later on."

When he questioned Janice, his whole manner changed, softened. You really couldn't blame the guy. Janice was looking particularly gorgeous at nine in the morning. Her blond hair fell smooth and straight around a face that didn't seem to have a touch of makeup on it. I knew, of course, it was invisibly helped with makeup base, subtle blush, undetectable mascara, and just the barest shine of pale lipstick on her full lips. She was wearing a sheer pale pink top with white jeans.

She smelled like freshly picked roses. The inspector was a gone goose.

"And you are . . . ?" he stammered.

"Janice Rogers, Inspector."

"Señora Rogers." He paused and smiled. Even her name delighted him. "Did you notice anything suspicious during dinner or afterward that might help us solve this murder?"

"Only that he was so rude and loud that everyone in the restaurant wanted to kill him, including the waiters and the chef," Janice said. "He complained about everything—the food, the wine, Spain, this trip. But you don't kill somebody for being rude, do you?"

"I can't imagine you killing anybody," the inspector said. "Except perhaps with your beauty." Ah, Spanish men. Why can't all men say things like that? He took her hand and gently brushed his lips across it.

I'm telling you, I would never have believed it in a million years, but Janice actually blushed. She did. People have been telling her she's beautiful ever since I've known her, but I've never seen anyone make her blush before. This devastatingly good-looking Spaniard accomplished it.

He tried to look as if he weren't affected by her, but failed. His face was much gentler, kinder than when he questioned the other passengers. "Will you be around later?" he asked. Evidently he had asked her all the hard-hitting questions he could think of.

"Of course," she said, not sounding like Janice at all, but like an ingenue in one of her plays.

The inspector left her reluctantly and made the rounds again, talking to some of the other passengers. He spent most of the remaining time with Denise and with two men I noticed in the restaurant who ate together and talked to each other as if they were a married couple. He also seemed to linger with Sylvia for quite a while, but I couldn't hear what he asked her. It wasn't from lack of trying, but the inspector's expression made it clear that I wasn't to get too close. He would stop talking and move away from me if I overstepped his boundary. I guess he didn't trust me, for some reason.

After about an hour, he headed for the door, and said, "Please remain on the train until further notice. I will be back with more questions when I have the medical examiner's report."

He left the train and Eduardo addressed the car full of passengers. "We apologize for the inconvenience," he said. "We have arranged for an excellent restaurant to bring the food to us as long as we are confined. We hope this delay won't last long. Thank you for your patience. If you will return to the dining car, we have prepared some breakfast for you."

He left the lounge car. There was an instant buzz of conversation in several different languages as everyone tried to understand what was going on. An uneasiness moved through the crowd as they returned to the dining car. I heard one woman say to her husband, "I think we should get our money back and go back home. This is ridiculous." It was beginning to sink in that someone, maybe the person right next to them, could be a murderer.

Gini's photography tip: Always offer to send the photo you take of someone to their phone or computer so they can see what they really look like.

Chapter 4

Whodunnit?

We attacked the buffet table like starving dieters. The array of croissants, coffee, tea, hot chocolate, smoked salmon frittatas, orange juice, and fresh fruit, was mouth-watering. We helped ourselves and sat down at the tables near the windows, where we could see police and reporters gathered outside. The other passengers were seated nearby. All of the tables were two-seaters because of the narrowness of the car.

I glanced around. The murderer could be anybody. There were several possibilities, but that's all they were—possibilities. And the killer might not even be one of my fellow passengers at all. It could have been someone in the restaurant. The inspector even suspected me. I must remember not to shoot my mouth off. Yeah, good luck with that, Gini.

"What do you think, Tina?" I asked when she sat down across from me with her hot chocolate and croissant. "The only one who is even a remote possibility as Shambless's killer is Sylvia. She hated him. Tom said that she was up late last night after he went to bed."

"Oh, Gini, that doesn't make her a murderer," Tina said, "I mean, I suppose she could have done it, but what about the blonde? What's her name? Julie. He certainly lied to her and double-crossed her. I don't think he brought her along to direct the film, do you?"

"She couldn't direct traffic," I said. "She's definitely a suspect."

"Let's see," Mary Louise said, from across the aisle, where she shared a table with Pat. "There's Danielle and Geoffrey and Michele—they didn't like him, but they don't seem the murdering type."

"Maybe Mike did it, Mary Louise," I said to tease her.

"Oh, Gini, come on," she said angrily until she realized I was kidding. "He brings lives into the world, not out of it."

"Well, it certainly couldn't have been that ridiculous, what's her name, Dora, who worshipped him," Pat said. "She'll probably kill herself out of grief."

"No, Dora is weird, but she couldn't kill a fly," I said. "She's too nervous. How about your new best friend, Denise?"

Pat glanced at me. "Oh, yeah, she's certainly a killer," she said. "She had no reason to kill him— at least as far as I know. But someone at the restaurant or somebody working on this train must have become angry enough to get rid of him. I can certainly understand that. That doesn't make sense, though. You can get really mad at someone, but you don't actually kill him. Only a crazy person does that. There has to be a better reason than anger at his rudeness and insulting behavior."

"Well, I hope that rude inspector is better at finding the killer than he is at asking questions," I said.

"He's not rude, Gini, he's adorable," Janice said, nibbling on some fresh fruit. "I hope he asks me more questions. I have lots of answers for him." She grinned wickedly.

"He's more adorable with some people than with others," I said. "He could hardly ask you any questions, he found you so attractive."

"You think so?" Janice said, reaching over to take a piece of Tina's croissant. "I didn't really notice."

"Right," I said. "You'd have to be a potted plant not to notice."

None of us resented the fact that Janice was the best looking in our group. She was an actress, after all. It was part of her equipment. Each one of us had something unique: I was the funniest, Mary Louise was the kindest, Tina was the smartest, and Pat was the wisest. We all felt we were lucky to have each other and treasured the special quality we each possessed. That didn't mean we didn't get on each other's nerves once in a while precisely because of the differences in our personalities.

Tom and Sylvia sat down at a table near us. Sylvia went to get some food from the buffet table.

"So, Tom," I said, "why did you do it?"

He laughed. "I bet a whole bunch of people killed him—you know, like that Agatha Christie movie where twelve people each took a turn killing the victim."

"My favorite movie," I said. "*Murder on the Orient Express,* right? I was thinking before, this dining car looks like it could have been on the Orient Express."

"That's the one. Someone should write *Murder on the Train in Spain,*" he said. "I can easily think of twelve people who would want to kill Shambless."

"Let's see," Sylvia said, coming back to the table with a cup of coffee. She looked even grayer in the morning. "Who would be on that list? There's you, of course, Gini, since you said you wanted to kill him. Every other woman on this trip is suspect, too, because he was always bashing women."

"How about you, Sylvia?" I said. Tina kicked me under the table, but I kept on. I couldn't help it. "I heard you used to produce his show and he fired you. Is that true?"

Sylvia glared at Tom.

"Do you have to blab our private business to everyone you meet?" she said to Tom.

"I didn't tell her that," Tom said. "She heard it from someone else. But it's true, Sylvia. Why deny it?"

"Because it's not something I want everyone to know. Even you should be able to understand that!"

This woman was a piece of work. I hated the way she talked to Tom and to everyone else. She was really making me mad. I know. It doesn't take much. But underneath I'm this gentle, sweet, kindly filmmaker. Believe that and I'll sell you the Brooklyn Bridge.

"Did he fire you?" I asked again.

"Not that it's any of your business," Sylvia said, "but actually, I resigned. I had good reason to leave. I couldn't stand the working conditions on that show. After I left, he made it impossible for me to get another job for a long time and—I don't want to talk about it." She wiped her mouth with her napkin and stood. "Are you coming, Tom?" she said as she was leaving.

"In a minute, Syl," he said. "I just want to finish my coffee." He watched her go. His face was so sad, I immediately regretted my hostility.

"I'm sorry, Tom," I said. "I shouldn't have done that."

"It's okay, Gini. Shambless made her life miserable and she hates talking about him. She didn't resign. He did fire her as producer of his show for no reason and spread the word that she was incompetent. Because of him she couldn't get another job in television for years. It was only through a friend of hers who was a sponsor of the soap that she got another producing job. Before that she worked as an accountant and as a restaurant manager. Shambless ruined her career. She really hates him."

"Enough to kill him?" I asked.

"Gini, cool it," Tina said sharply. "What kind of question is that to ask a man about his wife?"

"You're right, Tina," I said, chastened. "Sorry, Tom. Did Sylvia tell the inspector how she feels about Shambless?"

"No, of course not. She doesn't want him to know."

I didn't say anything. I felt, as usual, I had said enough.

Tom waved at two men entering the dining car.

"You have to meet these guys," he said. "I persuaded them to come on this trip," he said "They're friends from the old days in New York.

You know them, Jan—Mark and Sam who had that restaurant on West Forty-Sixth Street in the theater district. Remember?"

"They were great guys," Janice said. "Is the restaurant still there?"

"Ask them yourself," Tom said. He motioned to the two men again. They walked down the aisle to sit at the table in back of Tom's. Impeccably groomed, they made every other man in the car look like a slob. They each had expertly cut dark hair and a neatly trimmed mustache, and they were wearing immaculate white shirts and carefully pressed black pants. Their expensive loafers were polished to perfection. I'm no expert, but I think they were Pradas.

"Hoofers, these obviously guilty guys are Mark and Sam," Tom said.

"Don't joke, Tom," Mark, the older of the two men said. "The inspector thinks we are prime suspects."

"Why?" I asked. "You don't look like you could be guilty of anything except being too good-looking."

"I like you already," Sam said. "You're one of the dancers, right?"

"Yes, I'm Gini Miller. Hi, Sam. Tell us how that inspector could possibly think you did it."

"We worked to make gay marriage legal in New York," Sam said. "Shambless never missed a chance to condemn it. So it's simple: We must have killed him because he was anti-gay."

"Luckily," Mark said, "we were with other people all evening. After the restaurant, we were in the entertainment car watching you guys dance. You were really good. Then Carlos brought us coffee in our suite late at night."

"One of you could have slipped a little poison into his wine at dinner," Tom said.

"Right," Mark said. "Without anyone noticing in a crowded restaurant."

"That's ridiculous," I said. "We couldn't say anything because Eduardo asked us not to, but Shambless was dead before we danced last night. Eduardo told us just before we went on onstage. He wanted us to distract people so they wouldn't panic when they found out a passenger had died."

"You sure distracted us," Mark said.

"Now that we know you're not murderers," I said. "Tell us about your restaurant in New York. What's it called?"

"Mark and Sam's," Sam said.

"How did you ever come up with such an unusual name?" I asked, grinning. "What kind of food?"

"All kinds," Mark said. "French, Italian, Thai, Spanish. One of the reasons we came on this trip when Tom suggested it was to get some new Spanish dishes for the restaurant. You have to come and bring your whole crew."

"I got some recipes from the restaurant last

night if you want copies," Mary Louise said. "I'm going to try to make them at home, but I'd rather eat them in your restaurant."

"What did you get?" Mark asked.

"The seafood salad, the calamari, and the lobster with potatoes," she said. "You're welcome to them."

"Thanks. Which one are you again?"

"Mary Louise," she said.

"Bring your gang. Free meal on us."

"You'd love their restaurant, Mary Louise," Tom said. "It's elegant but fun. Everybody goes there."

"He's right. It's a terrific place," Janice said. "How are you two? I didn't know you were on this train. You look wonderful. It's been such a long time. How long has it been?"

"Since you and Tom were in *Virginia Woolf* together," Sam said. "We were always glad when you came into the restaurant after the play. You had such a good time together after beating each other up every night onstage. We couldn't believe how much you liked each other afterward. We always thought you two would get married."

"Yeah," Mark said. "We were surprised when you married someone else, Tom."

Mark opened his mouth to say something else, but Sam poked him. Sylvia was standing right behind him.

"Why were you surprised Mark?" Sylvia asked.

"Oh, did I say surprised?" Mark said, stammering. "I meant to say delighted."

Sylvia ignored him, and said to Tom, "Are you going to spend all day here? I've been waiting for you in the lounge car."

Tom's face was grim. He didn't look at us, just turned and followed her out of the car.

Nobody said anything until Janice saw the guilty expressions on Mark's and Sam's faces. "It's all right, guys," she said. "She's wound a little too tight."

I noticed Pat had returned to the buffet spread for more coffee and was talking to Denise. They brought their cups back and squeezed another chair in next to Mary Louise's.

"Okay," I said. "Why'd you do it, Denise?" I was kidding around. I wasn't prepared for her answer.

"My son was miserable because of him," Denise said, her face hard, unlike her usual cheerful demeanor.

"Oh, Denise, what do you mean?" I asked, shocked at her reply.

"He was a hateful man who did a lot of harm in this world," she said. "He opened his big mouth and spewed out lies that people took seriously. He never thought that his hatred and vitriol might have an effect on the people who listened to him. Cause them to do things."

"What kind of things?" I asked.

"He made ignorant people hate the same way he hated. His words made them bully people . . . other children . . . I . . ."

The look on her face was so tortured both Pat and I reached out to her.

"Denise," Pat said. "Tell us. What happened to your son?"

"I can't talk about it," she said, and stood up. She walked out of the car.

"I'm going after her," Pat said. "I think she needs to talk to someone. Maybe I can help." She followed Denise out of the dining car.

"I'm glad Pat went after her," Tina said. "She's clearly upset. If anyone can help her, Pat can. I noticed the inspector talked to Denise for a long time. Do you think she killed Shambless?"

"Who knows?" I said. "It seems unlikely, but what do we know? Maybe she did. She certainly had reason to kill him if she believes he was responsible for a problem with her son. I don't know what to believe anymore. It's really creepy being on a train with a murderer."

"Tell me about it," Tina said. "After our Russian cruise when someone got killed, I'd just as soon not go through that again." She shuddered.

"What is it about us?" Janice said. "This is the second time there's been a murder when we've been hired to dance somewhere. Two murders, in fact. Do you think we're a jinx or something?"

"Come on, Jan, don't exaggerate," I said. "There

weren't any murders on most of our trips. Anyway, I don't believe in jinxes. Speaking of dancing, Tina, are we still supposed to dance tonight? Or do we have the night off because one of the passengers was murdered? Is there a rule for this? Is there a clause in our contract that says, 'No dancing on days when someone is murdered'?"

"I'll find out," Tina said, laughing. She beckoned to Eduardo, who had just entered the dining car.

"Eduardo," she said. "Did you plan on us dancing tonight? It seems a little ghoulish to dance and sing as if nothing has happened. I know we did it last night, but are we supposed to do it again tonight?"

"Señora Powell," he said. "I know this is a lot to ask, but if you think your group would be able to dance for us this evening, it would help the other passengers a great deal. Several of them have already asked for their money back. They say they are leaving for home as soon as they can arrange a flight. I can't blame them. But your dancing might persuade some of them to stay. You bring such joy with your music. If you don't think you can do it, though, I certainly understand."

He looked at us, pleading silently for us to say yes.

"Of course we will, Eduardo," Tina said. "Okay with you, hoofers?"

Frankly, I could have done without performing that evening, but I wasn't going to let Tina down. I gave her a thumbs-up. The others agreed.

"That's what we're here for, Eduardo," Mary Louise said. "We'll do our best to distract the other passengers from the murder and mayhem."

"Thank you, my lovely hoofers," Eduardo said. "I don't know what I'd do without you."

"Should we do 'New York, New York'?" Tina asked.

"It's not very Spanish," Janice said.

"Have you been to New York lately?" I asked. "You hear Spanish spoken more than English."

Eduardo began to sing the words to "New York, New York" in Spanish in a mellow, lovely baritone. "*Nueva York, Nueva York.*"

My gang and I joined him, singing in English.

Passengers at a nearby table applauded. The mood of the day seemed to lighten a little. But like a lot of things in Spain, there was an underlying sense of foreboding, even while Eduardo was singing.

When we stopped, Eduardo said, "You're just what we need right now, señoras. Thank you."

"I think we need you, too, Eduardo," Tina said. "Would you sing in Spanish while we dance? It would be perfect."

Eduardo bowed. "It would be my pleasure," he said.

Such a lovely man, I thought. There's something about music that brings out the best in people. It's almost impossible to stay angry or scared or mean when you're singing.

Mike Parnell left the table where he had been sitting with Geoffrey, and walked over to say hello.

"That was great," he said. "I'm looking forward to seeing your show tonight."

"Mike, is there any news?" Mary Louise asked. "Did you hear anything? When can we get off this train?"

"Nobody knows anything for sure. It's all rumor. But the one thing they are positive about is that he was poisoned. They think it might have been one of the people who works in the restaurant or on the train."

He stopped, embarrassed, and said to Eduardo, "Of course I don't believe that, Eduardo. I know what a fine staff you have. It's just that Shambless was so rude to so many people, there's a slight possibility that one of them was angry enough to kill him. The police are questioning the staff now. Or someone in the restaurant could have poisoned his food. He certainly didn't make any friends there."

"Our employees are very carefully investigated before we hire them," Eduardo said. "None of them could possibly be a murderer."

"So you're saying it had to be a passenger or someone in the restaurant?" Mike asked.

"Probably," Eduardo said, then stopped, flustered. "I don't mean any of you, of course."

Michele, who had been sitting at the table with Mike and her father, got up and walked over to us.

"I know who killed him," she said.

Startled, we stopped talking and stared at this young woman, who looked so sophisticated in her white linen pants and bright coral blouse.

"Who, Michele?" I asked.

"It was the bartender—Juan," she said.

"Oh, Michele, what makes you say that?" Geoffrey said, coming over to join his daughter. "You shouldn't go around making wild accusations."

"It's true, Dad," Michele said. "I went into the bar car after we got back from the restaurant to get a chartreuse before the hoofers' show last night. Shambless was sitting there. He looked odd."

"What do you mean, odd?" her father asked.

"As if he were drunk. He was sweating a lot. He kept wiping his face with his handkerchief." Michele imitated him, swaying back and forth, pretending to mop her face.

"What makes you think the bartender killed him?" Geoffrey asked.

"I heard Shambless yelling at Juan because he didn't like the way he made his martini. 'Too much vermouth,' he kept yelling. He sounded totally drunk. He'd already had all that wine at dinner. Remember how much trouble he had getting into that car? He called Juan an idiot and said Spanish people were morons who didn't know how to do anything right. He grabbed Juan's tie and pulled him close. I thought Juan was going to kill him right then. His face was so angry. Shambless said he was going to get Juan fired for incompetency."

"Did anyone else hear this?" her father asked.

"Sure. There was a bunch of the train's crew cleaning up. They heard him—you couldn't help it, he was so loud. They looked like they wanted to kill him too. Most of the passengers were in the other car waiting for the dancers to perform. Oh, there was one passenger sitting at a table in the bar. I think her name is Sylvia something. She was watching Shambless and sipping a drink."

"You sure it was Sylvia?" I asked. "What did she look like?"

"Sort of gray all over. I remember her stopping at Shambless's table on her way out of the restaurant. She looked really fierce. I think that's why I remembered her."

"What happened then, Michele?" Mike asked.

"Shambless totally ignored me at first. Then he noticed me watching him. His eyes were all blurry. He sort of leaned toward me, and asked, 'Why aren't you in there watching the happy hookers? Don't you like to watch sluts dance?'"

Michele stopped and looked at us apologetically. "Sorry about that, hoofers," she said.

"What did you say?" I asked, ready to kill this man all over again.

"I said you were the happy hoofers, not hookers. I told him you were really good. I said he should go and watch you."

"What did he say then?" Tina asked.

"He said, 'When pigs fly.'" Michele said. "I wanted to get away from him—he was so disgusting. I thought he was going to throw up right there in the bar. Before I could get off my stool, he took a gulp of his martini and started yelling about how terrible his drink was. Then he sort of slumped over and leaned against the bar. Juan said perhaps he'd had enough. That made Shambless even madder, and he shouted, 'Don't tell me not to have another drink. See if you can make a decent martini for once in your life.'

"When I left, Juan was fixing him another drink, but he was really angry. His face was white. I wouldn't blame him if he killed Shambless."

"Juan would never kill anybody," Eduardo said. "No matter what Shambless did. He's a very fine man."

"I agree," Mike said. "He's been on this train for years."

"Michele," her father said gently, "I don't think you should mention this to anybody else. You could get Juan in real trouble. There's no proof that he poisoned Shambless."

"I guess you're right, Dad," Michelle said. "But if you'd been there . . ." She paused. "I certainly don't want to get Juan in trouble, though. I won't mention it again, counsellor." She smiled at her father. She obviously adored him.

"That's best," Geoffrey said. "Let's go back to the suite."

He put his arm around his daughter and they left with Danielle.

We were all silent, thinking over what Michele had said. It certainly seemed plausible that Juan could have killed Shambless. Spaniards are proud people. They don't put up with the kind of verbal abuse Michele just told us about. Juan had been a bartender for a long time, though. He must have heard worse than that from people who had too much to drink.

"I'm going back to the suite to get a book since we can't leave the train," Tina said. "Anybody coming with me?"

The three of us followed her back to our rooms, and knocked on Pat's door.

"Come on in," she said. "I want to tell you what Denise told me."

We crowded into her suite. Tina said, "We've all been wondering what she meant by 'My son was miserable because of him.' "

"It's so sad," Pat said. "Her son was very shy. He was no good at sports. The other kids in high school bullied him and called him gay. Denise thinks they did that because Shambless was always putting down gay people and ranting against gay marriage. She really believes he incited his viewers to violence against gays. She's convinced that's why her son was bullied at school and refused to ever go back there. He's in therapy now, and Denise blames Shambless for his depression."

"What did you say to her?" I asked.

"I told her that Shambless was a terrible person, but that he probably wasn't responsible for her son's behavior," Pat said. "A lot of bullying goes on in schools, unfortunately. Those kids who do it have probably never heard of Shambless."

"You're right, Pat," Mary Louise said. "Bullying in schools—especially in middle school but also in high school—is horrible. My kids said it used to go on all the time in their school. But the principal finally did something about it. She called in the parents of the bullies and convinced them of the harm their children were doing. They say it happens much less often than it used to. Thank God."

"I'm not sure how I can help Denise," Pat said. "She's distraught by her son's depression. She doesn't know how to help him."

"Where's her son now?" Mary Louise asked.

"He's with his dad. It's their scheduled time to be together. Denise said the father is good with the boy. She hopes some 'guy time' together will help the situation."

"Do you think Denise could have killed Shambless?" Janice asks.

"A couple of times when she mentioned his name, she did look as if she could have killed him. At least she wanted to kill him. I don't know why she talked to me about it. Maybe she wants me to find out. I wouldn't blame her if she did. I'm having a lot of trouble being sorry he was murdered."

"I think only that silly woman on the bus is sorry," I said. "That Dora person."

"She and several million people who listen to him every day," Tina said. "They call him up and tell him they are so honored to talk to him. They agree with every bigoted, nasty, rotten thing he says."

"I'll never understand those people," Mary Louise said. "They're always blatting on and on about all the welfare cheats lying around not working, living off the hardworking people in the country. Don't they realize there are little kids who don't have enough to eat, single mothers struggling to take care of their children, people with disabilities who would die without government help. Old people who—" She stopped. "I don't understand it."

"You're just a confirmed bleeding-heart liberal," I told her. "Like the rest of us. Anyway,

Tina, what's the schedule for the rest of the day? What are you going to do before our performance tonight?"

"I don't know what to tell you about the rest of the day because we can't get off the train. It's only eleven-thirty, so it's too early to drink. Who knows when we'll eat again? And there's nothing good on TV. I think I'll go back to our suite and call Peter. I haven't talked to him since we got on this train. He doesn't know about the murder."

"Everybody knows about the murder," I said. "Shambless's murder must have been in all the papers and TV at home."

"That's true. I wonder why Peter hasn't called me," Tina said. "Ever since the Russian cruise, he worries about me being surrounded by murderers."

"Maybe you haven't heard from him because he's on his way over here," I said. We all loved Peter because he adored Tina. Ever since her husband died two years ago, he has been trying to get her to marry him. He had been a good friend of Tina and her husband, Bill, since the two men were in law school together. Ever since his divorce he's done everything he could to make sure Tina was all right. She's still making up her mind whether she wants to get married again or not. Bill was a hard act to follow.

"I better call him," Tina said. "I miss him."

"I think I'll wander back to the lounge and see who's there and get some coffee," Mary Louise said. "Eduardo mentioned something yesterday about a cooking class on tapas. I'd love to know how to make them. Anybody want to come with me?"

Janice and I decided to follow her. We headed for the lounge car.

Gini's photography tip: Don't take a picture of someone chewing his food. It never looks good.

Chapter 5

My Tapas Is Your Tapas

"Eduardo," Mary Louise said. "Did you say something yesterday about a cooking lesson today? Tapas, I think you said. Is that still on?"

"I forgot all about it," Eduardo said. "Yes, the chef from a local restaurant will show us how to make the tapas you had yesterday. Come into the bar car. He's just about to start."

About two dozen women and some men, including Mark and Sam, were gathered around the bar where a chef in a toque was arranging ingredients in front of him. He was a plump, smiling man who spoke English with a lilting Spanish accent.

"Welcome, welcome," he said. "Come closer. I want to show you how to make one of the most popular tapas in our country—*tigres,* or stuffed mussels. They're perfect when people stop by late in the afternoon. *Mucho gusto.* Especially with wine. Very easy. Watch."

We crowded in closer to the bar. Mary Louise pushed me up to the front because I'm short.

"Okay," our jolly chef said. "I show you how to make *tigres* because someone here asked for them. Who was that?"

Mary Louise raised her hand and smiled at the chef. "Me. Guilty as charged, señor. I want to make them at home."

The chef took one look at our Mary Louise, looking unusually lovely this day in a turquoise sleeveless top and white jeans, and held out his hand.

"You must come and stand by me, so you will know exactly how to make *tigres,* or stuffed mussels as you call them."

Mary Louise was behind the bar before the chef could finish his sentence.

The chef put his arm around her and pulled her closer.

"So you won't miss anything," he said. He winked at his audience.

"I have done part of this recipe ahead of time. You must first steam the mussels until they open. Take them out of their shells and chop them up. Be sure and save the shells. You will need them later. Next you will see here in front of me, I have chopped up a leek, an onion, and a green pepper, which I have sauteed in olive oil until they are—what do you call it when you can see through them?"

"Transparent," Mary Louise said.

"*Si*, transparent," the chef said, kissing Mary Louise on the cheek. People are always kissing Mary Louise. She's so—kissable. "Then you add the mussels and a little white wine, around half a cup or more if you want to." He looked up and twinkled his eyes at his listeners. "I always want to."

He stirred the mixture for a couple of minutes and then added a chopped-up boiled egg, some salt, and tomato sauce. "You can buy the tomato sauce in your supermarket," he said. When he saw the look on Mary Louise's face, he chuckled. "Ah, a purist. Very well, my little American Julia Child, cook up your own tomato sauce if you want."

We applauded. Some of us were applauding Mary Louise's insistence on perfection. Some were applauding going to the supermarket for the tomato sauce.

The chef beamed. "You fill the mussel shells with this *excelente* mixture and then—"

"There's more?" a thin woman in our crowd said. "I thought this was supposed to be fast and easy."

"Compared to a paella, it is fast and easy," the chef said. "But you must be prepared to take a little time and trouble for something as delicious as this. Have you ever tried them?"

"Yes, I have," she said. "I ate a lot of them with my margarita yesterday. You're right. They're worth the trouble."

The chef looked happy again. "All right, ladies and gentlemen. The next step is a béchamel sauce, which I have already prepared. How many of you have made a béchamel sauce at home?

A few brave souls raised their hands.

"You are gourmets, no?" the chef said.

There was a mumbled "No," from those who had raised their hands. Mark and Sam were too modest to say that they made béchamel sauce every day at the restaurant.

"If you have made it before, you know that you heat some olive oil," the chef continued, "around four tablespoons. Add about three or four tablespoons of flour. Stir until it is smooth and add the cooking liquid from the mussels."

"You didn't tell us to save the cooking liquid," the annoying lady said.

"Mea culpa," the chef said, crossing himself. This guy was one-quarter chef, three-quarters comedian. I loved him.

"Well, just save it," he said. "Because you have to pour it into the flour and oil, and when it starts to get thick, you put in around a quarter of a cup of milk. Stir it all up, but don't let it get too thick. Got that?" He looked up at the snippy lady. She meekly nodded.

"Very good. Add some ground pepper and your béchamel is done. Spoon it over the mussels right away while it's still warm. Sprinkle some bread crumbs—or panko if you prefer a lighter crust—on top of the mussels. Now, you're ready for our final step." He looked mock sternly at the whiney lady. "Do you think you can stand one more step in this recipe?"

"If I must," she said.

"Is that what you say to your husband?" the chef, our comedian, said.

Some giggling was heard in the crowd.

"Simmer down," he said. "And concentrate. We are going to dip our stuffed mussels first in eggs and then in bread crumbs. Next, we turn our lovely mussels upside down and fry them in an inch and a half of olive oil. When your *tigres* are beautiful and golden brown, you take them out with forceps, drain them on paper towels. Then serve them to your guests, who will love you forever."

He passed them around to us to savor. The first one, of course, went to Mary Louise, who pretended to swoon at the first taste. "These are so good I think I'll take you home with me," she said.

"My bags are packed," the chef said.

Everyone chuckled as Mary Louise blushed.

"I will make something even better for you tomorrow," he said. "If you would like. Chicken paella?"

We all talked over each other promising to come back for the next lesson and wandered away from the bar savoring our *tigres*.

"Can I have a bite?" Mike said to Mary Louise as she left the cooking lesson.

"Help yourself," Mary Louise said.

Mike took a large bite and closed his eyes. "Are you really going to make these when you get back home?" he asked.

"But, of course," she said.

"Save a few dozen for me, will you?" he asked her.

I wondered if these two would meet again when they got back home. Was their attraction to each other just for the duration of the train trip or was there something more between them?

As if she had read my mind (happens all the time), Mary Louise said to him, "Mike, I'm so sick of this train." He wiped his mouth with a napkin. "I wish we could leave—just for a short time. I need to get some fresh air."

"I might be able to do something about that," Mike said in a low voice. He motioned to the three of us to follow him. Janice and Mary Louise and I hurried to catch up with him. When we were out of earshot, Mike said, "Don't tell anybody, but Javier asked me to have lunch with him at a great restaurant he knows. We have to take a boat to get there—it's in Asturias. He said I could bring you hoofers along if you want to go. Where's the rest of you? Are you guys up for this?"

"Of course!" Mary Louise said, practically dancing away. "I'll go get Pat and Tina. Don't go without me."

"Just Pat and Tina," Mike said. "We're the only ones allowed off the train."

"Did Javier say anything about—about any of us?" Janice asked, trying to pretend she didn't care.

"Yes, he said he was looking forward to seeing you again."

"Me? Or all of us?" she said, inspecting her nails.

"Well, what he actually said was, 'That tall, beautiful blond dancer, you know, I think her name is Señora Rogers. Oh, and her friends, too, of course.'"

Janice smiled. "Fantastico. Is that a word?"

"It is now," I said.

Mary Louise came running back. "They both said they just want to read and will see us later."

"Let's go," Mike said, and we sneaked off the train without anyone seeing us.

MARY LOUISE'S ADAPTATION OF THE RECIPE FOR TIGRES

Tigres

30 steamed mussels in their shells
2 tbsp olive oil
1 leek, chopped
1 onion, chopped
½ green pepper, chopped
2 hard-boiled eggs, chopped
½ cup white wine
2 tbsps. tomato sauce

Béchamel sauce:
4 tbsp olive oil
4 tbsp flour
½ cup milk
1 tsp black ground pepper

Breading:
2 cups panko
2 large eggs
1½ inches olive oil for deep frying

1. Chop mussels and save shells.
2. Saute leek, onion, and green pepper in 2 tbsp olive oil until soft.
3. Add mussels and white wine and stir for three minutes.

4. Add chopped eggs, and tomato sauce, and salt and mix in. Remove from heat.

5. Fill mussel shells with mixture

6. For béchamel sauce, heat olive oil in saucepan. Add flour and stir until flour is fried. Stir with whisk until smooth. While stirring, add reserved liquid from steaming mussels. Pour in milk, a little at a time until sauce is smooth and not too thick. Add ground pepper. Pour béchamel sauce over the mussel mixture in their shells.

7. Sprinkle filled shells with panko.

8. Dip the filled shells first into the beaten eggs and then into the panko.

9. Fill frying pan with olive oil and heat until medium hot.

10. Deep-fry shells until golden brown.

11. Drain on paper towel.

Enjoy!!!

Recipe for Chicken Paella

1 lb. spicy Italian sausage
3 tbsp. olive oil
½ cup sliced onion
½ cup sliced green pepper
½ cup sliced red pepper
4 large chicken thighs
¾ cup white wine
2 cloves minced garlic
4 cup chicken broth
½ tsp. saffron
1 tsp. paprika
½ tsp. coriander
1 bay leaf
½ tsp. thyme
½ tsp. oregano
Salt and pepper

1½ cup rice
¾ lb. raw shrimp, peeled
6 plum tomatoes, chopped
1½ cup green peas (frozen are fine)
¾ cup chick peas (you can use canned)
½ cup black pitted Kalamata olives
1 lemon quartered
Parsley for garnish

1. Simmer sausages in half an inch of water in a paella or deep frying pan for five minutes. Drain.

2. Slice the sausages and cook them in the oil until brown.

3. Stir in the onion, red pepper, and green pepper and cook until they are tender.

4. Take the sausages and vegetables out of the pan.

5. Brown the chicken thighs in the oil left in the pan.

6. Put the sausages and vegetables back in the pan with the chicken.

7. Add the next eleven ingredients listed above.

8. Cover and simmer for about half an hour.

9. Take the cover off the pan and bring all the ingredients to a rapid boil and add the rice. Don't stir it, just push it down with the back of a spoon.

10. When the rice rises to the surface and is about half cooked, add the next five ingredients. Reduce heat and simmer for about fifteen minutes until most of the liquid has been absorbed and the rice has finished cooking.

11. Garnish with lemon quarters and parsley.

Serves four very hungry people.

Gini's photography tip: Take pictures of people doing something, not just staring into the camera with fake smiles on their faces.

Chapter 6

Monkfish And Suspects

Javier was waiting for us in a van nearby. He was obviously looking for Janice and was clearly relieved when he saw her. Mary Louise, Mike, and I might as well have been invisible.

"This is so good of you, Inspector," Janice said. "It's a relief to get off that train for a little while. Thank you."

"My pleasure, señora."

He helped her into the passenger seat next to him. The rest of us scrambled into the back of the car.

"Don't you have a driver?" Mike asked.

"I'm not telling anyone about this trip," Javier said. "It might get back to the other passengers. I really shouldn't be doing this, but—" He looked at Janice again. "I hope you will forgive me, señora, but I didn't want you to miss this restaurant. It's just across this inlet in a place called Castropol in Asturias. The food is the best in Spain. I know the owner very well."

"You're forgiven," Janice said. "It sounds wonderful."

Javier was under her spell. She was especially beautiful that day. The gentle breeze ruffled the blond curls around her face, making her look about eighteen years old. He sat there without starting the car, just gazing at Janice, until Mike cleared his throat.

"Um, Javier, shouldn't we get going before anyone sees us," he said.

Javier pulled himself together, shifted gears, and started the van. We left the station and wound through the narrow streets into the little town of Ribadeo. Many of the buildings were white. They seemed to give the village a glow, a kind of purity. It was a Sunday morning and we could hear music coming from the church in the center of the square.

"Oh, Inspector, could we stop in that church for a minute?" Mary Louise asked. "I'd love to hear the music. I'm used to going to church on Sundays at home."

"They're expecting us at the restaurant, señora," he said. "I can't be away from the train for very long. I'd like to, but . . ."

"Inspector," Mike said in his usual calm, logical, quiet way, "it would only take about five minutes, and it would give these ladies a real feeling for the importance of the church, of religion, in Spain. It's not just a Sunday morning thing here. It's every day. It's deeply ingrained in people. Couldn't we just take a couple of minutes? I think it would mean a lot to Señora Rogers too. Right, Janice?"

Janice, who probably couldn't care less whether we went in the church or not, took one look at Mary Louise's face, and said to the inspector, "It would be such a great favor if you could do this. I don't mean to disrupt your plans, but . . ."

The inspector's face softened. I think Janice could have persuaded him to turn cartwheels in the middle of the plaza if she asked. He said, "Well, I don't see how a few minutes could hurt."

He parked the car near the church and we all got out.

"Be very quiet and follow me," he said.

He opened the door of the little church. The full beauty of the hymn sung by the choir embraced us as we entered. We stood in the back, trying to be as inconspicuous as possible. I hardly breathed as I admired the sculptures of saints around the sides of the church, the exquisitely carved crucifix at the front, the red-robed choir singing from the depths of their soul about their love of God, their faith in Him.

I'm not a very religious person. I was brought up Catholic but abandoned the organized part of my faith somewhere along the way. I talk to God when I need His help or when I'm grateful for the blessings in my life, but I haven't gone to mass for a long time. Standing there in this little church in Spain brought back all those Sunday mornings when I was a child, still an unquestioning believer, still sure that all I was taught was true. Now I question everything. I closed my eyes and let the music enter my soul, my heart, my whole body.

I could have stood there forever, but a gentle hand on my shoulder brought me back to this Sunday morning. "Time to go, Gini," Mike whispered. I started to follow him and the others out of the church, when I noticed a dark-haired woman kneeling in one of the pews. I could only see her back, but she didn't look like the other people around her. There was something different about her. Something American. She turned her face to the side for a second. I recognized her.

"Mike," I whispered to him, "Isn't that Denise Morgan over there in that pew?"

"Oh, it couldn't be, Gini," he said. "She couldn't have left the train without the inspector's permission. Must be somebody else."

I looked again. I was not convinced, but I let Mike lead me out of the church.

"Inspector," I said when we were outside again, "did you give anybody else permission to leave the train?"

"No one except you four were allowed to leave," he said. "Why do you ask?"

"Oh, I must be wrong," I said. "I thought I saw one of the passengers from the train inside."

"Not possible," the inspector said. I was sure it was Denise, but I let it go.

We got back in the van and Javier drove to the Eo River where a small boat was waiting for us.

"*Buenos días,* Hector," Javier called to the man on the boat. *Como estas?*"

"*Muy bien gracias,* Inspector Cruz," the man said. He was around sixty years old, his face weathered and lined by years of working outdoors. He reached out to help us climb aboard. Javier introduced us and asked Hector to take us to Castropol.

"We're going to Pena Mar for lunch," he said.

"The best food anywhere," Hector said.

"How far is it?" Janice asked.

"It's just across the river from Ribadeo," Javier said. "It will only take us about ten minutes. You can see it from here. Look straight ahead, señora." He put his arm lightly around her shoulders. "Do you see that little town perched on the hill—the one with all the white buildings and the white chapel at the top? That's Castropol."

Janice leaned back against him. "It's beautiful. I love all the white houses in this part of Spain."

The minute I stepped aboard that boat, I felt at home. I'm crazy about boats. Something about the water and the sound of gulls, the breeze cooling my face, the feeling of being away from real life for a little while was completely soothing.

"You are happy here, Señora Miller?" Javier asked, seeing the contentment on my face.

"I wish the trip were longer," I said.

I took out my camera and got some beautiful shots of the water and the gulls flying near us, the town as we approached it, of Ribadeo behind us.

In less than ten minutes, the boat pulled up to the pier. Hector helped us off and pointed to the winding road that led to the restaurant.

"Enjoy," he said.

"*Gracias,* Hector," Javier said.

We walked to the Hotel Pena Mar, stark white against the blue sky. The dining room was bright and sunny with a view of the beach and sea through the windows lining one side of the restaurant. The contrast of the blue sky against the white sand was so startling, I pulled out my camera again and took a quick shot of the view framed by the white curtained window.

"This is so beautiful, Javier," I said.

The owner greeted Javier with a welcoming handshake.

"Inspector, what a pleasure to see you again. *Bienvenido.*"

"Thank you, Enrique. I wanted these friends from America to taste your food. In fact, I couldn't let them leave Spain without eating here."

"I am honored you came to my restaurant," Enrique said. "I was afraid you would not come today because I heard there was some kind of disturbance on the train last night. What happened?"

"One of the passengers died under suspicious circumstances. He is a famous television star in the United States, so it's on the news everywhere."

"And you're here in my restaurant?" Enrique said. "How did you get away?"

"Nobody knows. I'll be back there soon enough. What do you have that's special today, my friend?"

"We have our salad of potatoes and tuna, one of your favorites. And for our main dish we have monkfish, just caught, fresh, white and flaky in our famous brown sauce. For dessert we have our creamy cheese mixed with honey."

"Perfect," Javier said.

"Perhaps you would like a nice dry wine, a Ribeiro with the monkfish?" Enrique asked.

"*Muy bien,* Enrique. A couple of bottles, *por favor.*"

The dining room was about half full. As we walked to our table, we could hear people talking and laughing, but the noise level was low. No raucous music or loud voices assaulted us. The whole atmosphere was relaxing.

When we were seated at a table near the window, Javier asked, "What do you think of our country?"

"Except for a murder now and then, it's really beautiful," I said. I couldn't help bringing up the subject on all our minds. I know, what else is new? "Who do you think killed Shambless, Inspector?"

"I'm not supposed to talk about that, as you well know, Gini." He lit a cigarette. "But as long as you brought it up, who do you think is the murderer?"

I started talking faster and faster as all the thoughts in my mind tumbled out disconnected, random, not at all logical, but I couldn't stop.

"Well, the most likely person seems to me to be the bartender because Shambless threatened to have him fired. Or it could have been somebody at the restaurant last night. Shambless was so rude." I tried to slow down, but it was no use. "Maybe it was that blonde who was with him. I heard them quarreling about something personal—it wasn't about the documentary. Then there's Denise who thinks her son was bullied because Shambless was anti-gay. Oh, and those two gay guys who own the restaurant—they hate him too. I almost forgot, there's Sylvia who worked for him until he fired her for no reason, or . . ."

"Or it could be you," the inspector said with a small smile. "Several people heard you say you'd like to kill him."

"Listen, Inspector," I said, "the only shooting I do is with a camera. And I have no idea how to get poison to put in someone's food."

"Gini talks like that all the time," Janice said, pulling her chair closer to the inspector's. "So far, she's never killed anybody. Anyway, she was with us every minute. We would have noticed if she said, 'Excuse me, I have to go kill Shambless. I'll be right back.' "

"Javier," the inspector said. "Please call me Javier."

He started to say something else to her, when the waiter brought us the monkfish Enrique had promised us. From the first bite, we were transported. The freshness of this dish, the exquisite taste of the creamy brown sauce that accompanied it, all fulfilled Enrique's description of this lunch. For a few minutes we couldn't talk. We just enjoyed every mouthful of this feast.

Javier looked around the table, pleased to see us devouring the meal with so much enthusiasm. He put down his fork, and said to Janice, "Let's talk about something else besides murder, señora. Let's talk about you."

The rest of us might as well have been eating lunch back on the train. The inspector concentrated his full attention on Janice. "Tell me about your life in the United States," he said. "Are you married?"

"Not anymore," she said. She seemed undecided as to whether to continue or not. Janice has never been one to hide her past, though, so I knew what was coming.

"I was married and divorced three times, Javier," she said. I could tell she said that to test him.

The inspector's expression didn't change. If Janice had expected him to leap out of his seat and shout "Wicked woman!" at her, she was disappointed.

Janice kept on going. It was as if she were driven to speak, determined to make her feelings clear. "Each of those marriages was a mistake," she said. "That's how I learned that it's important to live my own life and not to depend on a man to make me happy."

"What kind of man are you looking for?" the inspector asked, pulling his chair even closer to hers.

"I want a man who understands that I have a life of my own outside of loving him," Janice said, speaking passionately. "I don't want to live through him. I want someone who is as excited about my interests as I am about his. He has to understand that I love acting, that I'm most alive when I'm bringing a character in a play to life. I need someone who wants me to fulfill that part of myself as well as the part that loves him."

"Do you think you will ever find a man like that?" the inspector asked, looking directly into her eyes, which were a kind of blue-green this morning. They changed according to what she was wearing or the lighting in a room. She had on deep blue lapis earrings.

"I don't know, Inspector. Javier. Do you think I will?" she asked, her voice gentler than before.

"Perhaps I can help you find him," the inspector said, unable to take his eyes off her. It was clear he couldn't have cared less whether she had been married ten times.

A small sound from Enrique made him turn his attention to the restaurant owner.

"Try this Ribeiro, Inspector. See what you think."

Javier took a sip of the wine. "Perfect, Enrique," he said.

The inspector looked away from Janice reluctantly, as if he were suddenly aware that there were other people at the table too.

"Did you visit the cathedral in Santiago de Compostela before you got on the train?" he asked us.

"We did," Mary Louise said. "And we made a wish on that pillar—the one that has a shape of a hand that you wish on."

"What did you wish for?" Mike asked her.

"That my children would have happy lives," she said.

"No one gets through this life without trouble," Mike said. "But it has its moments." He looked at Mary Louise and smiled. "Like this one."

"I can't imagine how it could be finer," Javier said. "What did you wish for, señora?" he asked me.

"Well," I said. "I'm still hoping to adopt a little girl in India I met when I was filming a documentary about orphanages there."

"What a great thing to do," Mike said. "What are your chances? I know it's difficult in India."

I started to tell him about the obstacles in my way when Javier's phone made a noise. He glanced briefly at the text message.

"I am so sorry," Javier said, standing up. "But we have to return to the train immediately. There's a new development in the death of Señor Shambless. I'm afraid we'll have to go without one of Enrique's superb desserts."

We said our hurried thanks to our host and followed the inspector back to the boat.

Gini's photography tip: High noon is not a good time to take pictures outdoors. Try early morning or late afternoon for best lighting.

Chapter 7

The Plot Thickens

When we got back to the train, the platform was crowded with reporters and cameramen who surrounded our car. Javier struggled to open the door. When he pushed his way out, he couldn't move because of the reporters crowding him, hemming him in. Questions bombarded him from all directions, mostly in English and Spanish. It hit us again how famous Shambless was in our own country and, it seemed, in Spain too.

"Inspector, can you tell us what happened to Dick Shambless? Did somebody on the train kill him? Do you know who did it? Who was the girl he was traveling with? "

"We have no information at this time," Javier said. "We are waiting for reports from the medical examiner. I will be glad to answer your questions then."

He pushed his way through the crowd of reporters to get back on the train. We were still fighting to get aboard.

"Are you part of the train crew? What do you know about Shambless? Was he traveling with you?" Questions flew at us from all directions.

Mike cleared a path through the crowd for Mary Louise, Janice, and me. We just made it onto the train before the police slammed the door closed. We could hear shouts and noise still coming from the reporters as we reached the lounge car.

Eduardo had gathered all the passengers there. "Inspector Cruz will explain what is happening in a few minutes," he was saying as we entered the car. "Again, my apologies for this inconvenience and interruption in your trip. There will be no charge for drinks today."

My friends and I joined Pat and Tina at the bar where the free drinks were offered. Juan was pouring *cavas*, white wines and red wines, cosmos, margaritas, gin and tonics, and beer, efficiently and quickly.

"How was lunch?" Tina asked.

"Sssh," I said. "The inspector sort of spirited us out of here. He wasn't supposed to, but he couldn't resist the chance to be with Janice. The rest of us were just tagalongs. Great food. Monkfish with some kind of heavenly sauce. You and Pat should have come with us."

"I just couldn't face one more huge meal," Tina said. "I had a long talk with Peter. He was ready to get on the next plane when I told him about Shambless's murder. Somehow he hadn't realized it happened on the train we were on. He knew Shambless had been killed, but he didn't know where. He said, 'I should have known you and your gang would be involved somehow. I'm coming there. Next plane.' I managed to talk him out of it, but he wasn't happy about it."

"Why don't you just get it over with and marry him," I said.

"I'm thinking about it, Gini. Don't rush me. Much as I loved Bill, I'm enjoying the freedom of doing what I want when I want."

"How did the lunch with the inspector go?" Pat asked. "Did he fall madly in love with Janice?"

"Of course," I said. "What did you expect?"

"I don't know why I bother to ask," she said. "Hi, Denise. Come join us." She beckoned to her friend who had just come into the car.

Denise joined us and ordered a Kir from Juan.

"What's happening?" she asked. "No one will tell me anything."

"There's some new development in Shambless's death," I said. "The inspector is going to tell us what it is."

"A new development?" Denise said, pushing back a strand of her hair. "What do you mean?"

"We won't know until he tells us," I said. She seemed nervous, distracted.

I wasn't sure whether to ask her or not. Then again, when have you ever known me not to?

"Denise," I said. I couldn't go on. It seemed rude to continue.

"Gini?"

"Listen, Denise," I said. "Is there any chance you were in that little church in Ribadeo this morning?"

"Church, what church?" She was stammering. Not her usual calm, cool, collected self.

"I must be wrong," I said. "I thought I saw you. Obviously it had to be someone else." I was lying. I was even surer that Denise had been in that church after her reaction.

"You must be wrong," she said, pushing her glass over to Juan for another Kir. "Anyway, how could you have been in church today? Nobody was allowed to leave the train."

"We sort of sneaked in there," I said.

"Well, I wasn't there," Denise said, and moved away from me to talk to Pat.

Dora came up beside me, and said to Juan, "Do you have any tea?"

"Certainly, señora," he said, pouring her a cup of mint tea.

"Isn't it terrible about Mr. Shambless?" Dora said to me. "He was such a wonderful man. His voice will be missed. I don't know what the country will do without him. Oh, it's so sad."

Tina gave me one of her looks, but it didn't do any good. Once again, I couldn't stop myself.

"The country will be a lot better off without him," I said. "He was a loud, narrow-minded, dangerous, raving idiot."

"You must be one of those pinko liberals he was always talking about," Dora said, raising her voice, her face getting redder. "He was a saint. He spoke rationally while the liberal media raved on about gays and women's rights and the government paying for birth control. I used to watch him every day. I thank God that he came on this trip so I could meet him and get his autograph."

I felt Tina's hand on my arm, but I had already simmered down. I realized there was no way I could argue politics with this woman. I did want to find out more about her, though.

"Do you live alone?" I asked.

"I do now. My husband and I—we are no longer together. We had a daughter, but she died."

"I'm so sorry. What happened to her?"

"She was born with cystic fibrosis. She only lived until she was ten."

I tried to put a sympathetic hand on her arm, but she backed away.

"What kind of work do you do?" I asked. For some reason this woman fascinated me. I didn't know why. Something to do with my need to understand how people can have beliefs so different from mine, I guess. It's why I sometimes watched Shambless. A few minutes of him was enough and I changed the channel to something else, but I tried to understand.

"I worked as a secretary for a while," she said, "but now I'm retired. I spend a lot of time in my garden. You should see it. It's beautiful. I have azaleas and tulips, roses and rhododendrons. Just everything. It's a lot of work, but I enjoy it."

"It must be lovely. Where do you live?"

"In Florida. On Anna Maria Island. Mostly old people there, but it's comfortable and warm. I don't have to bother with people much."

"You don't like people?"

"Most of them are busybodies. Always butting into other people's business."

I looked at this thin little woman, talking too fast, her face twitching, her hands moving as she talked, pulling at her dress, fussing with her hair. I felt sorry for her. She was one of those people who was missing out on life, on all the miracles big and small that happen every day. She lived in a narrow little world weeding her garden and watching Dick Shambless. Now she couldn't even do that anymore.

Javier came back into the car. Everyone stopped talking.

"Señores and señoras," he said. "There is a new development in the death of Señor Shambless. The medical examiner has identified the poison that killed him. It was an extract from the oleander flower, which is extremely dangerous when consumed."

My mind flashed back to the vivid red oleanders around the restaurant we went to last night. I could picture them against the white wall. Somebody who worked there or ate there could easily have ground up some of their seeds or chopped up the leaves as a garnish on Shambless's salad. Who would ever know?

I assumed the investigation would shift to the staff at El Gusto del Mar and we wouldn't have to stay on the train anymore.

"Are we free to leave the train then, Inspector?" I asked him.

"I'm afraid not, señora," Javier said. "I still have a lot of questions to ask."

"How long will we be confined?" Geoffrey asked him.

"It's hard to say. Until we figure out who murdered him, I'm afraid."

"That could take forever. So many people disliked him."

"Including you, señor?"

"Well, I certainly didn't like him, but if I killed all the people I didn't like, the world would be a lot emptier—and a lot better."

There was a burst of laughter. It was a relief. A tension breaker. We needed that. Danielle gave her husband an appreciative glance.

"It has to be someone in that restaurant, Javier," I said. "There were oleanders all over the place. He made a total nuisance of himself throughout the dinner. Someone who worked there must have picked some oleanders and mashed them up in his food."

"I appreciate your suggestion, señora," Javier said. "I have already notified the owners to retain their staff for questioning."

"You should start with the chef," I said. "Shambless asked him if his steak was horsemeat. The chef was not pleased."

"You have a very strange idea about restaurants in my country, señora, if you think the chefs poison every customer who is rude," Javier said. "It's not a good way to get people to come back."

"He went beyond rude," I said.

"Thank you, señora," Javier said. I could see that he wanted me to shut up, so for once, I did.

"Señor Bergman," the inspector said to Steve, who was standing near him. "I would like to see what you filmed last night in the restaurant. Do you have your camera with you?"

"Afraid not, Inspector. After you questioned

me this morning, my camera was stolen. All the footage I filmed on this trip is gone."

The inspector spoke to one of his officers, "Domingo, search the train for Señor Bergman's camera."

Dora approached the inspector and tapped him on the shoulder.

"Yes, señora?"

"Inspector, I heard her say that she wanted to kill him because he was responsible for her son being bullied at school," Dora said, pointing to Denise.

There was an audible gasp from the passengers near her.

"And when exactly did you hear her say that?" the inspector asked.

"After you were here this morning, asking us questions."

"And you heard Señora—" He turned to Denise. She sat down quickly on the nearest chair. She looked very pale, as if she was going to faint.

"Are you all right, señora?" the inspector asked.

"Yes, Inspector," she said.

He turned back to Dora. "You heard Señora Morgan say that she wanted to kill Señor Shambless?

"Yes."

"Because of her son?"

"That's right."

"Did she say that to you?"

"No, she was talking to those two dancers." She pointed to Tina and me. "I wouldn't be surprised if one of them killed him either. They were always making nasty remarks to him and glaring at him while the poor man was trying to eat his dinner."

"You heard this woman, Señora Morgan, say that Señor Shambless was responsible for a problem with her son?" the inspector asked.

"I did. And she can't deny it. I was standing right next to her."

Javier looked at Denise.

"May I have a word with you in the next car please, Señora Morgan?"

Denise followed the inspector into the lounge car.

The buzz of conversation started up again. Dora tried talking to anyone who would listen. "I did hear her. I was right there. She did say that." The other passengers moved away from her. Dora scurried out of the railroad car, looking down at the floor, muttering to herself.

"I can't stand that woman," I said to my friends after she left.

"Just ignore her, Gini," Pat said. "She's one of those ultraconservatives. She worshipped Shambless. You're never going to agree with her or change her mind."

"You're right, Pat," I said. "But she got Denise in real trouble."

"The inspector will sort things out," she said.

"Speaking of the inspector, Jan, I hear he really likes you."

"I hope so," Janice said. "There's something about him that's very exciting."

"I wish he'd hurry up and solve this murder," Mary Louise said. "I want to get off this train and see this part of Spain."

"I might be able to persuade him to let us walk down to the beach together," Mike said to her. "It's beautiful. I've been there before. I want to show it to you."

"Oh, Mike, could you? I'd love that. Do you really think he'd let us go?"

"Let me see what I can do when he comes back after talking to Denise. Why did she say Shambless was responsible for her son's depression?"

I told him what she had told Pat.

"That poor woman. How terrible for her. She must have really hated Shambless."

"Who could blame her?" I said. "

"Look—Javier is coming back," Mike said. "Let me ask him. Wait here."

"Gini," Mary Louise said. "Do you think I should go?" Her face had a worried expression. Not her usual everything-is-fine look.

"You have to make up your own mind about this," I said. I wanted to yell at her, "Don't go! You'll be sorry if you do this." But you don't tell a grown woman with three children not to do something.

"I can't decide for you," I said. I couldn't stop there, of course. I can never shut up when I'm supposed to. "You're asking for trouble, hon. He really likes you. You don't want to lead him on, do you?"

"No, of course not. All we're doing is going down to the beach. What trouble could I get into there?"

My mind whisked me back to beaches on Cape Cod, the Jersey shore, and Florida where I got into plenty of trouble, but I didn't bring that up.

"I need to get away from the train for a while," she said. "All this talk about murder and poisoning and throwing up and death is getting me down." She looked so tired and sad. I wanted to tell her everything would be all right. But I didn't.

"I just want to talk to Mike and walk along the beach," she said.

"And . . ."

Mike came back. "Javier said we could go, but we should sneak out so nobody sees us," he said. "Oh, Gini, hi. Do you want to come with us?"

The look on his face said, " 'Please don't come.' "

"I think I'll stick around here, Mike," I said. "Go ahead. Have fun."

He looked so relieved I almost burst out laughing. They managed to steal out of the train without the reporters seeing them. I joined Pat, Janice, and Tina, who were munching some tapas at the bar.

"Hey, Gini," Tina said. "Where's Mary Louise?"

"Don't say anything," I said, putting my finger to my lips. "She went down to the beach with Mike. Javier said it was okay. Nobody is supposed to know."

"Javier seems to break all the rules," Janice said. "He gets more interesting all the time."

We watched him move from person to person, asking questions, listening, asking more questions.

"He seems smart," Tina said. "I wish he'd hurry up and solve this thing."

"What time are we going to dance tonight?" Pat asked.

"Eduardo said about ten," Tina said. "I think they're going to feed us about eight o'clock. Then we perform. Is everybody okay with the New York number?"

"What do we do about the part where we all line up and do kicks? Will we fit on that stage?" I asked.

"Let's go in there now and try," Tina said. "Michele can fill in for Mary Louise. All she has to do is kick. We can see if the stage is wide enough."

"I'm glad I lost that ten pounds," Janice said.

"So are we," I said. She punched my arm.

I saw that Javier had finished talking to Michele and her parents, so I ran over to them.

"Javier, is it okay if we rehearse in the next car? Do you have any more questions for us?

"No, go ahead, Señora Miller," he said. "I'm through for now."

I grabbed Michele's hand. "Michele, can you help us, please? We want to see if we fit across that dance floor for our 'New York, New York' number and we can't find Mary Louise. You said you wished you had the chance to dance."

"Are you serious?" she said. "I'd love to!"

"Okay if I watch?" Geoffrey asked.

"Come with us," I said.

I pulled Michele into the car with the dance floor and Geoffrey followed.

Gini's photography tip: Photographs of clouds are not good vacation shots.

Chapter 8

Have Another Orange Flan

"Could you show me a couple of the basic steps?" Michele asked.

"Why not?" Tina said. "The basic step is the time step, which goes like this. Stomp on your right foot—the whole foot stomps on the ground. Now hop on that same foot. That's it. Stomp, hop on the right foot. Now flap the left foot . . . that just means brush the ball of your foot back and forth once against the floor. Got that? Great. Then do a ball change. That's putting the ball of your left foot behind your right foot briefly and stepping down on your right foot. Try it."

Michele stomped, hopped, flapped, did a ball change and step the first time. She did it again faster, perfectly. She was having a great time. Stomp, hop, brush, ball change step. Faster and faster. Her shoulder-length dark blond hair moved with her, making her look even prettier than she usually did. Her blue and white skirt flipped around her long legs as she danced.

"You're a natural, Michele," I said.

"Okay, you've learned the time step," Janice said. "The basic step. Next time we'll show you the grapevine, the shuffle-off-to-Buffalo, the shim sham—all of them."

Michele beamed. You could tell that she loved every minute of this. I couldn't imagine anything so totally different from her career as an executive in a technology company and dancing on a train with the five of us. She reminded me so much of myself when I was in my twenties. Energetic. Enthusiastic. In love with life. I knew she would grab this world by its heartstrings and try everything it had to offer. I still feel like that, but it takes a little more effort now.

"Let's line up and see if this is going to work," Tina said. "Michele, all you have to do is kick from side to side. Easy. Ready, one, two three . . ."

We lined up, and with only inches to spare, we could fit on this floor, so close together we could feel each other breathe. Eduardo appeared and sang along with us in Spanish. In spite of all he had to do to restore some kind of sanity to this out-of-control train trip, he relaxed and let his voice reflect the fun of the music.

We kicked to the left and the right, higher and higher, like the Rockettes, really getting into it, laughing and singing along with Eduardo, "*Nueva York, Nueva York,*" in perfect sync with each other. Michele too. We danced backward, still in line, then forward, tapping and singing and having the time of our lives.

A few of the Spanish passengers cheered us on. "Brava. Brava," they yelled. They were soon joined by other passengers. Their enthusiasm urged us on to higher and higher kicks.

Javier walked in, his face animated as he clapped along with the others, and said, "*Olé.*"

"Is he adorable or what?" Janice said out of the corner of her mouth.

"Definitely," I said. I could certainly see how she was attracted to him.

We stopped, out of breath, and bowed. There wasn't a lot of room, but we managed somehow. Our performance was more intimate because of the narrow floor. You could tell that we loved dancing together and had fun doing it. It was contagious. The crowd was enjoying it too.

"That's just a preview of what you'll see tonight," Tina said to the people watching us. "Please come back at ten for the show."

They clapped and cheered us again.

Geoffrey came up and hugged his daughter.

"You were excellent, sweetheart," he said. "Did you have a good time?"

"Oh, yes," Michele said, her face glowing. "I want to do this forever. Think I'll go back home, quit my job, and join these guys."

"Come on, hoofer," Geoffrey said. "I'll buy you a Kir Royale. Juan makes a great one." He took Michele's hand and pulled her toward the bar. It did my heart good to see this man enjoying his daughter so much.

"Thanks, guys," Michele said, over her shoulder.

Javier could not take his eyes off Janice. You could tell he was trying to suppress his feelings, without any luck. He was hooked. Janice was so beautiful. Her face, which was always lovely, was glowing, slightly rosy, after the dance. She pushed back her hair, now curly and untamed. She looked so sexy, I knew Javier couldn't resist her.

"Señora—Janice," he said. "*Por favor.* Come." And he held out his hand to her.

As if mesmerized, Janice took his hand and followed him into the next car, looking back wickedly at us. Her expression clearly said, " 'Don't wait up."

"Hmmm," Tina said. "Looks like something is going on there with Janice and the inspector. What happened at lunch anyway?"

"He couldn't take his eyes off her," I said. "They definitely connected, Tina. We watched it happen over the best monkfish I've ever eaten."

"What do you think, Gini?" Pat asked. "Will she change to make him happy, or will he change to make her happy?"

"A little of both, I think, Madame Therapist," I said. "Janice is pretty sure of herself."

"So is he," Pat said. "He's Spanish, after all. Mucho macho."

Back in the lounge car, the other passengers were reading, sipping drinks, nibbling on tapas, and talking. Pat noticed Denise by herself at one of the tables. She was wiping her eyes with a tissue. "I'll be right back," she said, heading in Denise's direction.

"Well, Tina," I said. "What do we do with the rest of the day? It's only three-thirty."

"Let's go find Mark and Sam. I'd love to know who they think did this. They're fun to hang out with."

"Deal. I don't see them in this car. Let's ask Tom. He's a friend of theirs."

We found Tom sitting with Sylvia at another table in the lounge. She was writing postcards and he was reading a book on financial management. He looked up, happy to see us.

"Hey, hoofers," he said. "What are you up to? I'm bored. The Wi-Fi isn't working right now," he said. "I can't use my iPad. I don't know what the market is doing or what anything is doing. I feel like I'm living in another century."

"We're looking for Mark and Sam," Tina said. "We're bored, too, and they're always fun."

"I think I saw them go into the galley behind the bar," Tom said. "Come on. I'll help you find them. Want to come, Sylvia?"

"I don't find them as amusing as you do," she said. "Go ahead."

Tom looked like a little boy who had been let out of his room after a time-out. He almost skipped to the bar with us.

"*Buenas tardes,* Juan," he said. "We're looking for our friends Mark and Sam. Have you seen them?"

"They went in here, señor," Juan said. He opened the door behind the bar where there was a narrow kitchen. Mark and Sam were watching one of the staff cooking something creamy and delicious looking.

"Hey, Tom. Hi, hoofers," Mark said. "Come watch this. Ricardo is making a new batch of orange flans. He's got some already made and they are incredibly good."

"Can we watch?" I asked. "I love orange flan."

"Of course, señora," Ricardo said. "Come closer and I'll show you how I do this."

I don't ordinarily care much about cooking. I avoid it whenever possible. But desserts are different. I wanted to learn how to make a flan so I could cook it for Alex when I got home. Must be love.

Tina crowded in next to me. She actually likes cooking. Tom scrunched in behind us.

Mark and Sam made room for us to watch as

139

Ricardo explained each step as he went along. The counter was lined with ramekins.

"First you have to make a caramel sauce to put in the bottom of these ramekins. It's just sugar and water, but there's a trick to it. You put them in a saucepan and cook them for about fifteen minutes until the sugar is a nice brownish gold. Stay with it and shake the pan while it's cooking instead of stirring it. As you can see, it's just about ready now. I was cooking it before you came in."

We peered into the pot and could see this lovely caramelized sauce that was the color of Ricardo's hand, a yummy-looking golden brown.

"This next part is very important," he said. "You have to pour the sauce into the ramekins the minute it is done or the sugar will harden."

"Is it okay if I film you making the flan?" I asked, whipping out my camera.

"Certainly, señora. Could you send the film to my phone?"

"You got it," I said, and focused my lens on his deft hands.

He quickly and neatly filled each of the ramekins in front of him with the caramel sauce.

"Now you make the custard," he said. "You need both whole eggs and egg yolks." He broke the eggs into a bowl, separated some more eggs and put the yolks in the bowl, added sugar, and, using a whisk, beat them expertly until they were thoroughly mixed and frothy.

"Next," Ricardo said, "you add some orange juice—has to be fresh, none of that frozen stuff—some heavy cream, a little Grand Marnier and some vanilla, and stir until it's all mixed together in one delicious custard."

I was so hungry, I could barely keep filming this procedure.

"Just before you pour this into the ramekins, you add some orange zest and you're ready to bake these little beauties for about forty minutes in a 350-degree oven. You put them in a pan full of hot water that goes about halfway up the ramekins. I always test them after about thirty minutes because you don't want them to over-cook. They're ready when the top feels done. Not hard, just done. You can either serve them warm or put them in the fridge for a couple of hours and serve them cold. I have some here that I took out of the oven a half hour ago. Would you like to try them?"

I turned off my camera and eagerly took one of the ramekins Ricardo gave me. My first taste of this orange flan was so delicious I couldn't speak. So you know it was good. I can almost always talk.

"Ricardo, would you mind giving me the recipe for these?" Tina said. "My friend would love to make these for her husband."

We both knew Mary Louise would sacrifice her first child for a recipe like this.

141

"Certainly, señora," Ricardo said. "I'll have Carlos put it in your suite."

"*Muchas gracias,* señor," Tina said, cradling her little ramekin.

"*Por favor,* señora," Ricardo said.

"Let's go somewhere where there's more room and eat these," Tina said. Ricardo opened a door in the galley that led to the lounge car.

As we walked into the car, we saw Javier and Janice dancing to music coming from our sound system. He was holding her close, his face against hers. Her eyes were closed, she was smiling. If this had been a Hollywood movie, this would have been the last scene before the end. You knew they would live happily ever after.

Janice opened her eyes and waved to us, slowly, languidly, unhurriedly, as if she would never leave Javier's arms.

We stood there holding our orange flans, not sure whether to go back into the kitchen or into the next car. Sam said, "Uh, maybe we picked a bad time for dessert."

At this, we all laughed. Javier and Janice stopped dancing, but he kept his arm around her.

"We thought you might be hungry," Tina said, offering her flan to Janice.

"So thoughtful of you, Tina," Janice said. "As you can see, I was just longing for something to eat."

Javier's phone buzzed. He glanced at it and

kissed Janice's hand. "Something's up. I've got to get back to the lab. Will I see you later?"

"Yes, we're dancing tonight. Will you be there?"

"Of course. And maybe we can continue where we left off?"

Janice smiled. "Count on it."

When he was gone, I said, "Things are progressing fast, there, Jan. Looks good."

"Better than good," Janice said. "He took my hand and led me in here. Then he put his arms around me and kissed me." She smiled again "He's a really good kisser."

"Then what?" Tina asked.

"Then he said, 'I want to dance with you. I want to hold you.' I remembered that our CD player was in this room, so I turned on some music and he took me in his arms. It was as if we belonged to each other. Our bodies fit together perfectly. He's a sensational dancer. Better than anyone else. And he didn't say a word. Neither did I. We just danced and I never wanted it to end. Then you came with your desserts. Thanks a lot."

She wasn't angry. She just looked happy. Happier than I've seen her in a long, long time.

"It's good to see you like this, Jan," Tom said. Anyone looking at him could see that he wished he had been the one dancing with her. It was obvious that he still loved her.

Janice smiled at him. "Thanks, Tom," she

said. You could tell she wanted to say something more, but stopped herself.

"What happens next?" I asked.

"I don't care," she said. "I just want to go on feeling like this forever. You going to eat that flan? I haven't eaten for hours and I'm starving."

"You're in love," I said, reluctantly handing her my fantastically creamy treat.

"I'm just taking it one day at a time," she said. "But, Gini, he's so . . . so . . ."

"Macho?" I said, smiling at her.

"Yeah," she said. "Who knew that's what I wanted?"

"Enjoy, Jan," I said. "Listen, I'm going back to our suite and call Alex. I haven't talked to him since we've been in Spain. I don't have anybody to fool around with and it looks like it will be a while before we get anything else to eat. See you later."

Ricardo's Recipe for Orange Flan

Caramel sauce:
½ cup sugar
½ cup water

Custard:
4 eggs
4 egg yolks

¼ cup sugar
1½ cup orange juice (fresh)
1½ tbsps. heavy cream
½ tbsp Grand Marnier
¼ tsp vanilla
Zest from half an orange

1. To make caramel sauce, cook sugar and water together for fifteen minutes, shaking, not stirring, until golden. When done, pour into six ramekins right away so sauce won't get hard.

2. To make custard, whisk together eggs, egg yolks, and sugar until light and frothy.

3. Slowly add orange juice, heavy cream, Grand Marnier, and vanilla, and keep stirring until mixture is smooth.

4. Pour custard mixture onto the caramel sauce in each of the ramekins

5. Add orange zest to each ramekin.

6. Put ramekins in baking pan half full of hot water

7. Cook in 350-degree oven for about forty minutes. Test after 30 minutes. Tops should be barely formed, not hard.

8. Serve at room temperature or cool for a couple of hours and serve cold.

Serves six.

Gini's photography tip: Don't shoot people from below—it shows all their chins.

Chapter 9

Nueva York

On my way back to the suite, I noticed something on the floor in the corridor. I picked it up. It was a ring. I'd seen this ring before, but I couldn't remember where. It was shaped like a locket. When I opened it, I saw a picture of a little girl. A sad-faced child with dark hair and pale skin. Where had I seen this ring before? I put it in my pocket and went back to our suite.

I called Alex. He answered immediately. "Gini," he said. "I'm so glad you called. I've been thinking about you all morning. I was going to call you later. What's going on with Shambless's murder? I tried to get *The Times* to send me over there to cover the story, but they want me to interview the president about his meeting with Putin."

"Sounds fascinating, Alex. What an assignment!"

"Being bureau chief in Moscow came in handy. I'm now considered an expert on Russia. And I met you, which is even better. When are you coming home? I miss you."

"I'll be home in a few days. Can't wait to see you."

"Did they catch the murderer yet?"

"Not yet." I told him my theories about the possible suspects. "Which one sounds the likeliest to you?" I asked.

"Either the bartender or Sylvia," he said. "Just don't get hurt, Gini. Make sure there are lots of people around you at all times."

"Nobody wants to hurt me," I said. "But the inspector thinks I might have killed Shambless."

"What did you do now?" Alex asked, a smile in his voice.

"Oh, I just said I'd like to kill him because he was so obnoxious. Nothing serious."

"That's my Gini," Alex said, laughing at first and then his voice turned serious again. "Be careful, though, please. I don't know what I'd do without you. I love you."

"I love you too," I said.

Then it hit me. Right in the middle of our conversation I realized where I had seen that ring before. At the restaurant. Dora was wearing it when she asked Shambless for his autograph. That ring meant so much to Dora. She must be frantic trying to find it.

"Oh, Alex, listen, I have to go. There's something I have to do. I'll call you later and explain."

"Go, Gini," Alex said. "Do what you have to do."

"Good luck with your interview," I managed to say before hanging up, jumping off the bed, and leaving the suite.

I hurried along the corridor toward the lounge car. On the way, I heard a loud woman's voice coming from one of the suites, the door ajar.

"You've got to find it. Somebody stole it. I know it. I had it this morning. When I came back to the suite after the inspector questioned us, it was gone. It must have been Carlos who took it. Who else could it be?"

Eduardo's soothing voice said, "Señora Lindquist, Carlos would never steal your ring. Perhaps you dropped it on your way to the lounge car."

"No, I know I had it here in the suite. You have to search his room. Find my ring before he sells it."

I knocked on the door. "Excuse me, Dora," I said, pushing the door open. "I was passing by. I couldn't help hearing you say that you lost your ring. I found it on the floor of the corridor a little while ago. I was just about to return it to you."

Eduardo opened the door all the way, a relieved expression on his face. "Señora Miller," he said. "Thank you so much."

Dora elbowed him aside and grabbed my arm. "Where is it? What have you done with it? Give it to me."

I took it out of my pocket, puzzled at her frantic tugging at me. "Here it is, Dora."

She snatched it out of my hand, and said, "You took your time getting it back to me."

"I didn't remember that it was yours at first," I said, bewildered by her rudeness. "Then I recalled seeing it at the restaurant last night when you asked Shambless for his autograph. You said something about it having a picture of your little girl in it. That's how I knew it had to be yours. She's so pretty."

"You opened it?" she said, glaring at me. "You had no right to do that. Don't you know enough to respect a person's private property?"

"I'm sorry," I said, totally confused. "I didn't mean to . . ."

"Oh, never mind. Just go away and leave me alone."

Still in shock at her nastiness, I turned and left. Eduardo followed me and closed the door behind him. His face was anguished.

"I apologize, Señora Miller. It was so good of you to find her ring and return it. She was going to accuse Carlos of stealing it. He's never stolen anything in his life."

"I know, Eduardo. I heard her. That's why I knocked on the door. I didn't want her to get Carlos in trouble. She certainly was upset. I guess it's because her daughter died and the picture of her in the ring is very important to her."

"That's no excuse for the way she acted, señora. Thank you very much for your help."

"You're welcome, Eduardo. Are you still going to sing when we dance tonight? You have a beautiful voice."

"I look forward to it. We will be eating about eight. We're getting the food from a fine restaurant in Ribadeo. I think you'll be pleased."

"You're amazing, Eduardo. You've handled these past two days superbly. I can't imagine you've had much practice supervising a group of tourists after somebody has been murdered."

"I've learned through the years to deal with the unexpected, señora. I must admit, this was the most difficult to manage. *Muchas gracias.* I'll never forget you and your marvelous hoofers. You've helped me through the worst part."

"You can believe we'll never forget this trip," I said.

I headed back to the lounge. Mike and Mary Louise weren't back yet. I looked at my watch. Six o'clock. If she was going to eat before the show and get dressed, she should be back soon. Mary Louise was as reliable as Big Ben.

I thought about my friend Mary Louise, whom

I met at *Redbook*, where we both worked as editors right after I got back from studying photography in Paris for a year. We were both still single. She insisted that I drive with her and Tina from New Jersey to California and back in a ten-year-old Pontiac on a triple-AAA route that took in all the major must-sees in our country. I couldn't resist her. It's very hard to resist Mary Louise once she makes up her mind about something.

We rode mules down narrow trails into the Grand Canyon, took pictures of Old Faithful geyser in Yellowstone National Park, marveled at Mount Rushmore, had drinks at a revolving bar in San Francisco. We plugged up the holes in the water hose in our old car with bubble gum, and drove through rain and fog. We saw everything and became fast friends forever, through my divorce, her marriage to George and her three children, the death of Tina's husband. It cemented our friendship for the rest of our lives. I can't imagine my life without those two. They're like my sisters.

I met Janice later when she moved next door to me. We bonded right away. I'm drawn to people who are different, who live by their own set of rules. As an actress, director, and triple divorcée, Janice more than qualified.

Pat was one of Janice's closest friends and so, of course, became one of mine too. She was one of those people who think outside the box—my

favorite kind of person. She was also a therapist
and helped me with a lot of my problems when I
was trying to decide whether to get a divorce or
not.

I ordered a *cava* from Juan and was drawn to
the spectacular view from the window of the
train. I could not get enough of the beauty of
this part of Spain. Rugged and impressive, the
Picos de Europa mountains rose on one side of
us, while the ocean glistened on the other. The
sea always speaks to me, makes me feel peaceful
and part of it. I took a sip of my drink and noticed
Shambless's companion, Julie, sitting nearby. She
was playing some kind of game on her iPhone,
looking totally bored. She was wearing another
of her low-cut tops that showed why she didn't
have to have much of a brain.

"May I join you?" I asked.

"What for?" she asked. I almost walked away,
but something made me stay. Was she just a ditz
who was all cleavage and very little brain, or a
steely-minded murderess who took vengeance
on a man who betrayed her? I sat down across
from her.

"I thought you might want someone to talk
to," I said.

She glanced up briefly, her expression telling
me she had no interest in talking to me at all.

"About what?" she asked.

"I don't know," I said, sitting down next to her.

"About Dick Shambless maybe. At the restaurant you seemed to like him a lot. And then, not so much."

"Right," she said, and lit a cigarette. "What business is that of yours? I don't even know who you are."

"Sorry," I said. "I'm Gini Miller. One of the dancers."

"Oh, yeah," she said. "You were the one who was snotty to Dick at dinner."

"Have you known him a long time?" I asked.

"Not really. I met him through Steve, you know, the camera guy. I used to be a model."

"How did you get into directing films?" I asked. "I'm interested because I make documentaries too."

"I'm not really . . ." She paused. "A director. I work for Steve in his studio, booking clients, modeling—anything he needs doing. Like that."

"So Shambless was one of his clients?"

"Yes. Shambless hired Steve whenever he needed publicity pictures. He got the idea to do this film about Spain because it would be a free vacation for him. He asked me to come along. To get funding from the network, he called me his director."

"You and Shambless seemed . . . oh, sort of . . . uh . . . close. I mean for someone he just met recently."

She looked away, and then back at me. "Like I

said, that's really none of your business, is it?" She started to get up.

"I didn't mean to be so nosy," I said. "You're right. It isn't any of my business, but the inspector seemed to . . . oh, you know . . . He seemed to think you might have had a reason to kill Shambless. I thought maybe I could help."

She sat back down. I had her full attention. "You really think he suspects me?" she said. She leaned forward. She stubbed out her cigarette. "Well, see, Shambless thought it would be fun to take me along on this trip," she said, talking fast. "I was really dumb. I thought it was more than that. He talked about leaving his wife for me. Said I was just the kind of girl he wanted to spend the rest of his life with." She laughed without mirth. "And I believed him."

"You must have liked him a lot," I said, not meaning it, wanting her to talk more about him.

"Who could like him?" she said, wrinkling her nose. "I thought I'd have a good life with him. You know, travel, nice clothes, contacts. I told you—I was dumb."

"So what happened?"

"In the restaurant he kept putting me off, not wanting to talk about us. I realized he was never going to leave his wife. He was just gonna have a good time with me here in Spain and then dump me when we got home. He was a total jerk." Her face was twisted in anger.

"What did you do after that?" I asked. I felt like one of those detectives on *Law & Order: SVU.* Mariska Hargitay, maybe. I always liked her. Maybe because she was Jayne Mansfield's daughter and she grew up to be such a good actress.

"When we left the restaurant he wasn't feeling well," Blondie continued. "I tried to take care of him when we got back to the train. I followed him into the bar, but he told me to leave him alone."

"What did you do?"

"I left him alone," she said, her expression hard, her voice tough. "Just like he asked." She stood up. "If you're through with your interrogation, I'm getting out of here."

She left the car.

I was trying to figure out whether she had the guts to kill him when Mary Louise came toward me. She sat down across from me, smiling.

"Was that Shambless's cutie you were talking to? What's with her?"

"She's no devoted fan of his, I'll tell you," I said. "She actually thought he was going to leave his wife for her."

"So you think she killed him?" Mary Louise asked.

"I don't know," I said. "She could have. She was mad enough. Where have you been? Where's Mike? Did you go to the beach? How was . . ." I looked at her glowing face as she started talking in a low voice, fast and eager, the words pouring out of her as if she were sixteen years old.

"Oh, Gini. It was . . . It was so romantic. We talked as if we had known each other forever. He talked about Jenny and how much he loved her. He said he didn't think he would ever meet anyone he felt the same way about again. And then he took me in his arms. I didn't mean for it to happen, Gini. He kissed me. He said I was beautiful. He said he couldn't help it, but he loved me. We were walking by the water, the rocks towering over us. It was as if we were all alone in the world. It was lovely."

"What did you say to him?"

"I said . . ."—she reached over and grabbed my hand—"I said I loved him too. When he kissed me I wanted him to keep holding me forever. It was as if we were meant to be together. What am I going to do?"

I put my other hand over hers and leaned forward. I was worried about this friend I loved like a sister. "Honey," I said, "as we said before, Mike is very vulnerable. He misses his wife. You look like her. I can certainly understand why he loves you. But you're feeling neglected by George. Mike is lonely. You're in a romantic country in the middle of a murder investigation. It's like a movie. But you're not Meryl Streep! You can't make any final decisions now."

"I know you're right, Gini. But his arms around

me, his kisses, the way he looked at me, I wanted it to last forever."

"What did you decide?" I asked. "You didn't promise anything, did you?"

"No, not yet." She looked over at the bar, caught Juan's eye, and signaled for a cup of coffee. "Mike went off to talk to Javier to find out if there's anything new in the investigation," she continued. "I'm so glad you're here. I really needed to talk to you."

"You know I love you, Mary Louise. And I know George has a lot of faults. But you love him—and you have children. You can't throw it all away for a few minutes on a beach in Spain. I'm just asking you not to make any promises now that you'll be sorry for when you get back home."

"I'll try, Gini. Thanks. You're such a good friend."

"How many times have you steered me in the right direction, Weezie?" I said, using a nickname she hated. "And I'm not talking about which road to take in California."

She laughed and took a sip of my drink.

There was a disturbance at the bar. Eduardo was talking to Juan, who was obviously upset. Juan said in a loud voice, "Why do they want to talk to me?"

"They just want to ask you a few questions," Eduardo said. "It's nothing to worry about. I'll come with you." He put his hand on Juan's arm, but Juan shrugged it off angrily.

Eduardo saw us watching them. He spoke softly to Juan in Spanish and they left the bar car.

"What's that all about?" Mary Louise asked.

"It sounded like Juan is a suspect," I said. "They certainly can't think he did it."

"It's hard to believe," she said. "But remember what Michele said. She thinks Juan was angry enough to kill Shambless because he threatened to have Juan fired. She heard Shambless. She saw the look on Juan's face."

"Juan's worked on this train for years," I said. "I'm sure he's met lots of people as rude and obnoxious as Shambless."

"I know, but Shambless was especially irritating. He would drive anybody to murder—even you," she said.

"Especially me," I said. We raised our glasses to each other.

Mike came into the car and pulled up a chair at our table.

"What are you two beautiful women talking about now?" he asked.

We told him about Juan. He was immediately serious. "Juan is no killer," he said. "I'd swear to that in court."

"Michele seemed to think he was guilty," I said.

"No one took her seriously," Mike said. "Shambless was rude to everybody. Everyone hated him except that fan of his, what's her name . . . Dora?"

"She's a weird person," I said. I told them the story of the ring and her reaction to my finding it. "But I feel sorry for her. After all, her little girl died. The child's picture was in that ring. No wonder Dora was frantic at losing it."

"What happened to her daughter?" Mary Louise asked.

"Dora said she was born with cystic fibrosis and only lived to the age of ten," I said. "It's obviously very painful for her to talk about. She didn't even want to show the picture to Shambless in the restaurant when he asked to see it."

"She certainly adored him," Mary Louise said.

"Passionately," I said. "I don't understand it, but she worshipped the ground he walked on."

Eduardo came into the car looking distraught. His usual calm, reassuring manner was gone.

"Eduardo, are you all right?" Mike called out to him. "What's happening?"

"Oh, Señor Parnell," Eduardo said, coming over to us. "It's terrible. They've arrested Juan. I know he didn't do it, but several people heard Shambless yelling at him. They said they heard Juan say he wanted to kill him. But it's not possible. He would never kill anyone. I've known him for years."

"Does Inspector Cruz think he did it?"

"He must think so or he wouldn't have arrested him. Anyway, the inspector said we could continue on the train trip. I feel terrible leaving Juan here—like I'm deserting him."

"Does he have a lawyer?" Mike asked.

"Yes, I made sure he has a very good one."

"Then there's nothing more you can do right now," Mike said, putting a reassuring hand on Eduardo's arm. "You can keep in touch with his lawyer and find out what's going on. If you have to, you can come back here."

"I guess you're right, Señor Parnell, but I don't like it."

I felt so sorry for this kind man who cared about every member of his staff. I knew he felt like he was betraying Juan by handing him over to the police. I tried to think of a way I could help.

"Do you still want us to dance tonight, Eduardo?" I asked.

"It would be wonderful if you could, Señora Miller. But if you'll forgive me, I don't think I can sing as you requested."

"Of course, Eduardo," I said. The guilty look on his face broke my heart. "Just come and watch us and maybe you'll feel better. I'm so sorry about Juan. I don't think he did it either."

"Thank you, señora. He's a fine man and I know he will be cleared."

He bowed to us and went into the next car.

* * *

Our "New York, New York" outfit was quintessential Liza Minnelli. We wore black tights, a white tuxedo shirt, and a black jacket that came to the middle of our thighs. I don't mean to brag, but we looked sensational. Dancing has kept us tight and slim. Flat stomachs, great legs, and energy to light up the sky. Two blondes, two brunettes, and me the flashy redhead. Our performances on trains and cruise ships—even in local community centers and retirement homes— were the most fun we've ever had.

Tina turned on the classic Sinatra version of "New York, New York." We burst onto the dance floor, linked arms and kicked to the right and the left, swung into our tap routine, dipping, lunging, grapevining, time stepping, flapping, and shuffling off to Buffalo. We brought all our energy, our love of good old New York, New York, the city that doesn't sleep, chasing our blues off the train out into the sea crashing below us, the Picos de Europa mountains rising above us. Dancing with our hearts, as well as our feet, we brought all the joy and fun of America to this northern Spain, narrow-gauge railroad trip. There was nothing narrow-gauge about our moves. Even on a small floor we managed to cover every inch of it to celebrate our city, our America, our love of life.

When we finished, again the crowd jumped to its feet to cheer us, clapping and shouting, "Brava," and "Way to go, Hoofers" and "More, more, more." For a few minutes we had lightened the mood of the people on this train and taken their minds off the murder, even if only briefly.

Javier, in the front row, tried to remain impassive, but he failed as he looked at Janice. He clapped and cheered and reached out to lead her from the stage.

I heard him say, "You were incredible. You are beautiful. That was so . . . so joyous, what you did. So American."

Janice smiled at him. "Do you see why I love it?"

"I'm beginning to," he said. "It consumes you, fills you with happiness. It's the way I feel about my work. It's so intense when I'm working well and everything is coming together."

"Like this murder case?" Janice asked. "You really think you've found the right man?"

He hesitated, looking troubled. "I hope so. He had the motive—hatred of the victim. He had the opportunity. He could have poisoned his drink. He just doesn't seem like the kind of person who would commit murder. He's being questioned now. Thanks to Eduardo he has a good lawyer who will help him."

"And then what?" I asked, butting in the way I always do.

"And then we have to find the real murderer," he said. "Why don't you confess, Gini? It would save me so much time and effort."

"All right," I said. "I did it. I ran outside the restaurant, crushed up some oleanders, and sprinkled them on his salad after he ordered steak and French fries. I've decided to become a vegan. If there's anything I can't stand, it's a steak eater."

Even Javier squeezed out a small laugh at that.

"Will the train be able to continue on this trip?" Janice asked.

"For now," Javier said. He looked at her as if he never wanted to let her out of his sight. "I want to show you my Spain. It's so beautiful, this part of Spain. You have to see more of Asturias and Cantabria and San Sebastian. I want to hold you and make you love my country the way I do."

He realized we were all around him. He stopped, looked at me, and said, "And you, too, of course, señora."

"Do you really want to hold me?" I asked, teasing him.

"I want to embrace all of you happy hoofers," he said. "You were really superb tonight. You will allow me to make love to all of you?"

Sounded like a good idea to me. "We're all yours, Javier," I said, opening my arms to him. "Take us."

"You'll have to fight me for this one," Mike Parnell said, coming up to put his arm around Mary Louise. "She's mine."

Mary Louise took his hand. "Come dance with me in the next car, Mike. I'm still high from our show."

They left, and Pat said, "What's going on with Mary Louise, Gini?"

"I think she's getting in deeper than she means to, Pat," I said. "I'm worried about her. I think she's caught up in the excitement of this whole situation—the train, the murder, a very vulnerable, attractive man who is paying her the kind of attention she wants from George. She isn't thinking about what will happen when the trip is over."

"Do you think it would help if I talked to her?"

"Definitely, Pat. You're good at showing her how to sort things out. She'll listen to you. I've tried to get her to be careful, but she doesn't really believe me. I know George is difficult—but I think she loves him."

"I'll see what I can do," Pat said. "Listen, Gini, there's something else I have to talk to you about. It's really worrying me. You're the only one I can tell this to."

"Of course, Pat. Let's go back to your suite where it's quiet and talk."

Tina was talking to Mark and Sam. We waved to her and headed out the door. As we left the car, we saw Dora leaning over a wheelchair talking to the boy we had noticed in the dining car the day before.

"Wonder why he uses a chair," I said.

"He has muscular dystrophy," Pat said. "I was talking to his mother earlier. I told her I'm a therapist. She wanted to ask me about his little sister. The mother worries that she isn't paying enough attention to her daughter because she has to spend so much time with her son."

"What did you tell her?"

"I said that every parent of a child with a disability worries about their other children in the same way. I told her about something I heard of recently called SibShops for the siblings of people with disabilities. It's a place where they can play and talk about their resentment or anger or guilt and it stays right there. It's led by a trained therapist. They play with other children with the same feelings. SibShops are all over the country. I told her I'd find out where there was one in her area."

"How long do children live with muscular dystrophy?"

"It depends. But they don't usually live to adulthood," she said.

"That's so sad," I said.

We opened the door to her suite and sat down to talk.

"So, tell me. What's up?" I asked.

"This is very hard, but I know you won't judge me. That's why I wanted to talk to you."

"Whatever it is, Pat, it's not going to change our friendship."

Pat looked out the window at the lights of the little town down below.

"It's Denise," she said. "I think I have . . . feelings for her."

"What do you mean, feelings? You're sorry for her? You sympathize with her? You . . . Oh—you mean . . ."

"Yes, I'm attracted to her."

I've always known Pat was gay. She's never made any secret about it with us, her friends. Although she's had affairs, she's never found anyone she wanted to be with permanently.

"You mean, you're serious about her?" I asked.

"I'm not sure, Gini, but she's not like anybody else I've ever met. I don't know what it is exactly, but I want to get to know her better."

"You're sure? I mean . . ." I stammered. "What if she . . ."

"Killed Shambless? Oh, Gini, Denise could never kill anyone."

Skeptic that I am, I wasn't that sure. Pat wanted so desperately to believe it, that I said, "Well, I hope you're right. But what did you want to ask me about? You seem so worried."

"We've talked about her son a great deal. One

time I hugged her and she clung to me. Then she kissed me. I mean a real kiss, Gini, not a small peck on the cheek. We both knew there was something going on."

"What happened then?" I asked. Pat had never really talked to me about her affairs with women. We've discussed everything else on earth, but she never told me any details about her love life. Pat is more private than the rest of us, perhaps because she had to keep the most important part of her life a secret while she was growing up. Before she accepted it herself.

"Nothing. We pulled apart, but we looked at each other and we knew. We wanted each other but were afraid to go further. Gini, I don't know what to do. It's against all the rules of therapy to fall in love with someone you're counseling."

"But she's not a patient. She's just someone you're trying to help. What's wrong with going further?"

"It's not that it's wrong," she said. "It's that we're both afraid to really get any more involved in case it all falls apart. If it's just physical. If we . . ."

"Listen, Pat," I said. "That's true when anybody falls in love. We never know if it's for real or if the other person will love us the way we love them. But it's worth it. It's always worth trying. I didn't know if Alex and I would last when I met him on that Moscow river cruise. It could have been a lovely interlude, a short affair. But it wasn't.

It lasted. Or at least it's lasted until now. We'll see when I get back. Give it a chance, honey. See what happens. If nothing else, you'll make each other happy for this train trip. If it keeps on after you get home, that's even better. Of course, there is the small problem that she might be a murderer."

Pat looked at me and smiled. Her whole body relaxed. "I just don't believe that. You're the best, Gini. I'll see what happens. Denise is a wonderful person. I'd like her to be in my life, even if only for a little while. Thanks so much. I think I'll go find her."

"You'd better wait until tomorrow—it's late." I yawned and opened the door to her suite. "I wonder what happened to your roommates."

"Yeah, where are they?"

"I have a pretty good idea. I wouldn't wait up for them. Anyway, sweetie, I'm going to bed and I'll see you in the morning."

"Thanks, Gini. I feel much better. You should have been a therapist too."

"Oh, right. Until I started yelling at some poor person who didn't do what I told him to do. I don't have your patience and understanding,"

She chuckled. "Night, Gini."

When I opened the door to our suite, Tina was just getting into bed.

"Hey, Gini. Where is everybody?"

I told her about Janice and Mary Louise.

"I'm glad somebody is having fun," she said. "I wish Peter were here."

"I know what you mean," I said with a sigh. "I miss Alex too."

"It's only for a week," Tina said. "Then, watch out."

I turned out the light.

Gini's photography tip: Be careful of backgrounds. Don't let your photo show a tree sprouting out of someone's head.

Chapter 10

What Were You Thinking?

I was almost asleep when someone knocked on our door. The knocking grew louder. I heard a woman's voice say, "Let me in."

I jumped out of bed. Tina woke up, and said, "What is it? What's going on? Who's there?"

I opened the door. Julie Callahan, Shambless's "director," was standing in the corridor wearing the same blouse and skirt she had on when I talked to her earlier in the day. She was shivering, though it wasn't cold.

I pulled her into the room and wrapped my robe around her.

"Julie, what's the matter?" Tina said. "What's happened?"

"It's Steve," she said, her teeth chattering, barely able to talk. "Oh, it's terrible." She collapsed on my bed and started to cry.

"Julie, tell us," I said.

"He's dead," she said in a muffled voice. "I went to his room just now. We were going to have a drink together, but he didn't come to the bar, so I went to his room. I knocked and there was no answer. I opened his door—it wasn't locked—and I saw him lying on the floor. He had thrown up all over the bed. It was a mess in there. I tried to wake him, but it was no use. I didn't know what to do, so I came here. I'm sorry to wake you, but I . . ."

"You didn't call anyone? Eduardo or Carlos?" I asked. I didn't mean to speak so sharply, but I couldn't help it. What was she thinking?

"I was afraid they'd think I did it," she said. "You told me they already suspect me of killing Shambless. And I was in Steve's room. I didn't know where else to go but here."

When she saw the look on my face, she said, "Forget it. Sorry to disturb you. I'll go back to my room." She started to open the door and leave.

"No, don't go," I said. "I didn't mean to yell at you. Come back in and sit down. I'll go find Eduardo and tell him what's happened."

"Are you sure?" she asked.

I wasn't sure of anything at this point. Should I shove her out of our room and call the police? Did I become her accomplice if I let her stay with us?

Tina rescued me. She's always the voice of reason. "Gini, go find Eduardo and tell him what happened. I'll stay here with Julie until the police get here."

I left the suite and ran down the corridor toward the lounge car.

Luckily, the train was not moving. It was always stationary at night and traveled during the day while we were exploring some town or historic place.

It was almost midnight, so I didn't expect to find Eduardo still awake. I should have remembered how hardworking he was. I found him in the dining car checking on the tables to make sure they were set up properly for breakfast.

"Señora Miller," he said, surprised to see me. "Are you all right?"

"No, I'm definitely not all right, Eduardo," I said. "Steve—you know Steve—the photographer who was with Shambless—he's dead. Julie found him in his room. She didn't know what to do so she came to our room. When she told me about Steve, I came to find you."

"Dios!" Eduardo said. "Go back to your room, señora. I'll call the inspector immediately."

I went back to our suite. Tina, Julie, and I

looked out the window until Javier and his officers arrived within minutes and climbed onto the train. A medical team pulled up in back of the police cars and followed them.

I opened the door of our suite cautiously. The police and medics were running toward Steve's room. Other passengers, awakened by the noise and lights, opened their doors. We could hear "What's the matter? What's going on?" in several different languages.

Our unflappable Eduardo walked up and down the corridor reassuring people, telling them to go back to sleep, calming them down, not mentioning that someone else was dead. He just said, "Someone was sick and the medics have come to take care of him."

Julie sat on the edge of the bed, still shivering. "Can I stay here with you?" she asked. "I don't want to go back to my room. What shall I do? They'll think I did it. I was the one who found him."

"No, they won't, Julie," I said. "They'll want to ask you a few questions, but they won't think you did it."

I was just talking, saying anything to reassure her, but I knew they would certainly suspect her at first. When I looked at Tina, it was obvious she thought the same thing. As usual, Tina took over. She's always good in a crisis.

"You can stay in here with Gini," she said to Julie. "I'll bunk in with Pat. There's at least one empty bed in her suite tonight. And don't worry. Everything's going to be all right."

She gathered up her things and left the suite.

I looked at Julie. I didn't know whether she was going to kill me next or if she was innocent. I thought, *What if she did kill Steve? What if she killed Shambless because he wouldn't marry her? Then Steve found out she did it, so she killed him too.* I could be in the same room with a murderer.

A loud banging rattled our door. I opened it and the inspector pushed me aside and confronted Julie.

"What happened?" he asked.

Julie told him about finding Steve.

"And you came here instead of reporting his death to the police, or Eduardo, or somebody in charge?" he said. I had never seen him like this, coldly angry and accusatory.

"I was scared," she said. "Gini said you suspected me of killing Shambless. I was afraid you'd think I killed Steve too. I didn't know what to do. I just ran and came here."

"You reported a death on this train to a couple of dancers?" the inspector said.

"I told you, I was so upset, I didn't know what I was doing."

"They're certainly the first people I'd come to if I discovered a body lying on the floor in a train," Javier said.

Julie shrank under his sarcasm. She appeared to be on the verge of tears.

"What did you do when she told you what had happened?" he asked me. "Decide that you would solve this murder by yourself?"

"I ran to get Eduardo and told him to call you," I said, standing up to my full five-feet-three and looking him in the eye.

The inspector addressed Julie again. "Did the victim say anything to you earlier that might have given you a clue about who would want to kill him?" Javier asked.

"No, he just kept talking about his camera," she said. "It was gone. Somebody stole it. It had most of the footage for the documentary. He was going crazy."

"But you didn't discuss with him why someone would steal it?"

"Well, he did say there might have been something on the film that would give a clue about who murdered Shambless, but he couldn't remember anything suspicious," Julie said. "He was taking shots of the town and the restaurant and the passengers on the bus. I think he thought somebody stole the camera because it was expensive and they were going to sell it. Somebody who worked on the train, maybe."

Javier motioned to one of his officers.

"Please go with this officer, Miss Callahan," he said. "I want to ask you some more questions at headquarters."

"But I didn't kill him," Julie said. "I just found

his body. He was my friend. Why would I kill him?"

"You're not a suspect, Miss Callahan," the inspector said. "I'm not accusing you of anything. I just want to talk to you in a more private place."

Julie straightened up. "Let's get this over with," she said.

She left our room and was escorted off the train by a police officer.

Javier looked at me.

"You were going to let a possible murderer spend the night here in your suite?" he said. "Gini, what were you thinking?"

How do I get myself into these things? I wondered. I'm bopping along making films, dancing on cruise ships and trains, perfectly happy, and all of a sudden I'm the sneaky person in a crime scene!

"Hold it, Javier," I said, calming down a little. "I ran to tell Eduardo the minute she came in here and told us what happened. I wasn't going to throw her out of our room at a time like that."

He looked at me and shook his head. "You're lucky you're still alive," he said. "Good night."

He left. I tried to sleep that night but didn't have much luck. I tossed and turned and wrestled with the events of the night, trying to figure out what I should have done, what I did wrong. As usual, I blamed myself for not doing the right thing. Whatever that was.

* * *

The next morning Tina and Pat knocked on my door. They came in and sat on the bed.

"Where's Julie?" Tina asked.

I told her about the inspector's visit.

"I've never seen him like that," I said. "He was furious at us for taking Julie in, Tina. What were we supposed to do, tell her to go away when she had just found Steve's body?"

"Or killed Steve," Tina said. "She could have killed him, Gini."

"If she had killed him, would she have come here?" I asked.

"She probably thought it was better than going to the police," Pat said.

"So she's at police headquarters now?" Tina asked.

"Yes," I said. "Not under arrest, Javier said. Just for questioning."

"Sounds like arrest to me," Pat said. "I can't believe there was another murder on this train. Shouldn't we go back home before one of us ends up dead?"

"I feel like we've been through all this before, said all this before," I said.

"Think Russian river cruise," Tina said. "People were murdered on that trip too. What is it about us?"

"We're like flypaper," I said. "Only we attract murderers instead of flies. I'm going to the dining car to find out what's happening. Want to come?"

"We'll meet you there," Tina said.

I dressed quickly and headed for the breakfast buffet.

Javier was there waiting for the other passengers to show up.

"Javier," I said. "What's happening?"

"Gini, go get some coffee and sit down somewhere," he said. "I have to tell the passengers what has happened and then check with the medical examiner."

"Where's Julie?" I asked.

"We've released her for the time being," the inspector said.

Javier saw my expression and gave me a gentle push toward my friends. "Relax, Gini," he said. "I'll arrest you later."

I hoped he wasn't serious, but you never know with Javier. I joined my gang.

The dining car soon filled up with all the other passengers, sleepy-eyed and anxious as they poured coffee and nibbled on pastry that Eduardo had supplied.

We found Mike and Mary Louise at one of the tables holding hands. They were talking to each other as if there were no one else in the world, no one else in the car. Mary Louise looked up as we approached her table. "Hi, guys," she said. "What's happened? What are you doing here so early?"

"Steve—you know, Shambless's camera guy— was killed last night. They found his body in his room."

"You're kidding?" Mike said. "I wonder why Eduardo didn't call me. I'll be right back." He went over to Javier and talked earnestly with him for a couple of minutes.

When he came back, he said, "At least we know it wasn't Juan. Couldn't have been. He was in jail. They'll have to let him go now."

He sat down across from Mary Louise again. "Looks like we're stuck on this train. I wanted to show you Luarca. It's a little fishing village, all white houses and blue sea and little boats on the water. You'd love it."

"How can you even think about sightseeing?" Mary Louise said, her loving expression turning into annoyance. "Who cares about white houses and little boats? Someone just got killed. Another person on this cruise is dead." She got up and left, clearly distraught.

Mike watched her leave the car. When he turned back to us, he said, "She's . . ."

"She's married, Mike," I said, sitting down across from him. "Stay a minute, will you? I want to talk to you."

Pat and Tina headed for the buffet table.

"You don't have to tell me, Gini. I know she's married. But she doesn't really love her husband."

"You don't know that," I said. "I've known her

179

all the time she's been married to George—
twenty years now. Every marriage has good times
and bad. She does love George, but when she left
for this trip, he was inattentive and distracted by
business and worries about his job. Then she
came on this trip and met you—attractive, attentive, vulnerable, needing someone to love again.
Mary Louise looks like your wife."

"But I wouldn't have fallen for just anybody.
Mary Louise is bright and kind and interesting
and beautiful. She's fun to be with. She's . . ."

"She's like Jenny," I said.

He nodded his head. "Yes, I know. She's the
first person in a long time I can imagine spending the rest of my life with."

"Think, Mike," I said, trying to talk calmly. I
tend to talk too fast and too excitedly when I'm
upset. This time I knew I had to sound logical,
reasonable. I cleared my throat and continued.
"She has three children. Think what a divorce
would do to them. Her whole life would be dis-
rupted. George really does love her. I know he
doesn't show it all the time, but what husband
does? I just don't want to see her get hurt."

"I know you mean well, Gini, but I love her."

He stood up, put both hands on the table,
and leaned closer to me. "And I'm not going to
let her get away."

He left the car just as Janice came in and
walked over to my table where Pat and Tina had
joined me.

"Missed you last night, Jan," Pat said.

Janice smiled. "I know, Pat. Javier took me down to his boat. We were having the best time drinking *cava,* talking, when they called him about midnight and told him to get back to the train immediately. That there had been another murder. We rushed back here."

Janice looked a little rumpled, but beautiful just the same. Wish I could do that.

"Isn't he perfect?" she said.

"Whatever happened to 'Me strong woman, You supportive man'?" I asked. I can't help it. I just say these things.

"With him, it doesn't matter," she said. "I want a man who takes charge, watches over me, keeps me safe. Especially a man who looks like that."

"Are you sure you're Janice Rogers?" Tina said. "The Janice Rogers who wants to live her life her way, who doesn't want to live through her man? The woman who always says, 'I am woman, hear me roar.' That Janice Rogers."

"I used to be her," she said. "But I've decided I don't really want to roar. I just want to purr. However, right now I want to snore. I'm going to go take a nap."

"Don't wake Mary Louise," Pat said. "She was out all night, too, and is probably asleep in your suite."

"Our Mary Louise?" Janice said. "Our sweet little housewife married to rotten George? Mary Louise who never does anything wrong?"

181

"She hasn't done anything wrong—yet," I said. "But she's getting close. And incidentally how, uh, wrong did you get last night?"

"None of your business, my dear."

I wish people would stop saying that to me.

Javier went to the front of the lounge and rapped on the table to get everyone's attention.

"Señores and señoras, I'm afraid I must ask you to stay on the train for a while. There has been another murder."

Some of the passengers gasped. Some said, "Another murder? What kind of a train is this?" "I'm getting out of here while I'm still alive." Some sat down and put their heads in their hands.

Javier waited until the noise died down. Then he said, "Steve Bergman, the photographer who was working with Shambless, was found dead in his suite last night. It looks like he was poisoned the same way Señor Shambless was, with oleander poison. If any of you has information about Señor Bergman, if you saw him last night after the dance performance, if you can tell us anything at all, please let me know right away."

Nobody said anything at first. We all looked around the room, not meeting each other's eyes. Finally, Dora stood up and confronted the inspector.

"Why don't you ask that blond girlfriend of Mr. Shambless?" she asked. "I don't see her. Wasn't she sleeping with that photographer? Why don't you ask her a few questions?"

"I'm right here," Julie said, walking into the car, her hair uncombed, no makeup, her clothes wrinkled. "Anything else you want to ask me, Inspector?"

"No, I think we're finished for now, Miss Callahan," the inspector said. "But please remain available for further questions when we have a more thorough report from the medical examiner."

Julie pushed her hair out of her face, and said, "Yeah, be sure and let me know if you find any oleander powder in my room."

Geoffrey, who had been listening intently to this exchange, spoke to Julie.

"Excuse me, Miss Callahan," he said, "I'm a barrister. If I can help you, please let me know."

"I don't have any money," Julie said.

I could have punched her. Geoffrey wasn't some ambulance-chasing, sleazy little lawyer looking for work. He was a highly respected attorney in England.

"You don't need any," he said. "Just consider this my good deed for the day."

Julie's face softened a little. "Thank you," she said. "I would be grateful for your help."

"Why don't you come into the next car and we can talk," Geoffrey said. She followed him out of the lounge car.

"The rest of you are free to go," the inspector said. "But please be available if we need you." He singled me out of the crowd and pointed to me.

"Especially you, my little American detective," he said.

"Anything you say, my pompous little Spanish inspector," I muttered to my friends.

"Gini, cool it," Pat said. "We don't want to have to bail you out of a Spanish jail."

"Javier," I said to the inspector, "Does 'free to go' mean free to leave the train? I need some fresh air."

"Yes, you may go, Gini." the inspector said, "But be careful." He looked genuinely concerned.

"I'm going to get my camera and walk to that white town they keep talking about—Luarca," I said to my gang. "Want to come?"

"I'm just going to eat," Tina said. "A nice leisurely breakfast with lots of calories. Then I'll join you. See you later, Gini. Try not to get arrested."

Pat motioned for me to go by myself and she joined Tina.

**Gini's photography tip: Not everyone wants to
see thirty-seven pictures of your grandchild.**

Chapter 11

Give That Doggie Another Bone

I grabbed my camera and walked toward the sea. As I got closer to Luarca, I understood why people call it the Villa Blanca, or white city. Everything was white, shining in the sun, bright against the blue, blue sky. White houses, a white chapel high on a hill, even white steps leading down into the town.

Near the ocean, the contrast of the startlingly bright blue water against the sand and the palm trees around the sea begged to be photographed. I had my point-and-shoot camera with me, so I didn't need to worry about speed or distance. I tried to capture each part of this blue and white town in its own frame.

Walking along the shore, I found little yachts and fishing boats side by side, all different colors, yellow and red and green against the blue of the water. A man with a bright red shirt stepped out on the deck of his boat just as I took the picture. That's the sort of serendipity that makes me love photography. If you wait long enough, the perfect photo just appears.

When I'm looking at something through a camera, it's as if I'm inside the camera. I see a mountain or a cathedral or the ocean the way the camera sees it. I keep trying until I get exactly the angle, the composition of the picture, that is going to make the best photograph or segment of a film.

With new cameras, so different from the ones I learned on, I can see immediately whether I got what I wanted. I don't have to wait until the photos come back from the lab. If I didn't get exactly what I wanted, I can try again. It's very exciting to me. I forget everything else when I'm doing it.

As I focused on one of the craggy rocks at the water's edge, a man moved from behind them. It looked as if he were pushing something down into the sand. I couldn't see clearly what it was. I zoomed in on his face and realized it was Mark, one of the restaurateurs. I waved to him, but he didn't see me. He disappeared around one of the other rocks. My camera could no longer find him. He was probably just exploring the seashore. But what was he burying in the sand?

I shot the beach and the town from every angle until I had exactly what I wanted. I strolled to a café nearby for a cup of tea. There was only one other customer—a man in his twenties wearing sunglasses. He was very good-looking with blond wavy hair, tanned skin, strong hands. A golden Labrador lay curled up at his feet. I love dogs and couldn't resist reaching over to pat the Lab. Then I noticed that the dog was wearing a harness. He was a guide dog.

"Hi there," I said. "Is it okay if I pet your dog?"

"Sure," he said. "He isn't working at the moment, so go ahead. I'm Jonathan, by the way, and this is Hawkeye."

I reached over and took his hand. "Hi, Jonathan. I'm Gini Miller. Your dog is beautiful."

"He is my best friend. It's okay. You can pet him and talk to him. It's only when he's guiding me that it's not all right. It's hard for sighted people to understand, but a guide dog has to concentrate on his job when he's getting me somewhere. Talking to him or petting him distracts him."

"Are you from the train?" I asked. "I don't remember seeing you. I certainly would have remembered Hawkeye."

"No, I'm here by myself. I always wanted to come to this part of Spain, so I decided to spend my vacation here."

"Where do you work?" I asked.

"In Boston," he said. "I work at the Statehouse for a Massachusetts senator. Thanks for that question. Most people assume I couldn't possibly have a job."

"My cousin is blind," I said. "She's an accountant in a tax office. She has a talking computer, talking iPad, talking everything. She gets furious when people assume she couldn't possibly be working in an office, or anywhere for that matter. Your job sounds fascinating. What do you do?"

"I'm the liaison between the senator and callers who ask for advice about health care or government funding. I was lucky. It's not easy to find work when you're blind."

"How did you do it?"

"Right after I lost my sight—I was in my last year of college—I volunteered to work at the Massachusetts Office on Disability in Boston. I didn't want to leave that city. I had a lot of friends and I love it there. I testified before the senator's committee to try to get more funding. She hired me to work in her office."

I reached down to scratch Hawkeye's ears. He nuzzled my hand and his intelligent brown eyes accepted me as a friend.

"Isn't it hard traveling by yourself—especially in a foreign country?" I asked.

"I'm not by myself. I have Hawkeye. The only tough thing is that people often seem to think I lost my intelligence when I lost my sight. They get nervous and don't talk to me in the same way they did when I could see. You get used to it. You mentioned the train. Are you traveling on it? I wanted to take that trip, but it was too expensive."

"It is expensive," I said. "But I'm one of the entertainers, so it's free for me. I'm having a great time— except for a couple of murders."

"I heard about that," Jonathan said. "Can't say I was sorry about Shambless's death. You seem fairly calm about it. What do you mean you're an entertainer?"

"I'm here with four friends. We dance on the train at night and get to see this beautiful country during the day. We're called the Happy Hoofers. I have no idea how we got hired, but I'm glad we were. I could do without the murders, though."

"Do they know who did it?" Jonathan asked.

"Not yet. There are several suspects."

"Let me get this straight," Jonathan said. "You're dancing on a train with a murderer lurking about. Aren't you a little nervous?"

"Not a little," I said. "A lot!"

"Wish I could be there when you dance," Jonathan said.

"Why not?" I said. "The train stays in the station at night, so you could come to the show tonight—you and Hawkeye—and have a drink with us afterward. I'll arrange it."

"Thanks—what's your name again?—Gini. I'd love to do that."

I looked up and saw Michele coming toward me. She bent down to let Hawkeye sniff her hand.

"What a beautiful dog," Michele said. "Is it all right to pet him?"

She looked so pretty in her jeans and a yellow shirt, her face without a line or mark in the bright noonday sun. I wished Jonathan could see her.

"Help yourself," Jonathan said. "We've been neglecting him."

"Jonathan, this is Michele," I said. "She's on the train with us. Michele, meet Jonathan. He works at the Statehouse in Boston."

"What do you do there?" she asked.

He told her about his job with the senator. "How about you?" he asked.

"I'm in San Francisco," she said. "Computers."

"Anything new that talks that I should know about?" he asked.

"As a matter of fact," Michele said, sitting down next to him, "there is. You'll love this, Jonathan. I'm working on start-ups in wearable technology. There's a new one you have to get."

She reached down and scratched Hawkeye's ear.

"Tell me about it," Jonathan said.

"It's a very small camera that attaches to eyeglasses."

"That's not exactly new," Jonathan said, sounding disappointed.

"Wait," Michele said. "It also talks! Really. You point at something and it tells you what you're pointing at."

"You're kidding," Jonathan said. "Talking glasses?"

"It's incredible," she said. "You point at a menu and it reads it to you. Point at a traffic light and it says, 'It's green.' In the grocery store, it tells you the brand and the product—you know, 'That's Kellogg's Corn Flakes.' Turn the box around and it reads you the ingredients."

"You mean there's a talking component attached to the camera on the glasses?" Jonathan asked, his voice rising with excitement at this new technology.

"Exactly."

"It probably costs a fortune, right?" Jonathan asked.

"It's expensive," Michele said, "but you could probably get the senator's office to pay for it. It would help her as well as you."

"How do I find out more about this?" Jonathan asked.

"Can you come to the train later on?" Michele said. "I'll give you all the information then."

"I'm coming to hear these murder-prone hoofers tonight. I'll talk to you then."

I still cannot believe how far technology has

advanced in the last decade. I always feel one step behind.

"Gini," Michele said, "I'm feeling guilty about Juan, and I wanted to ask you about it. Was I right talking about that conversation I overheard between him and Shambless? Should I have kept it to myself? He's in jail because of me."

"Michele, listen to me," I said. "He wasn't arrested because of what you said. They found some oleander leaves in his room. Somebody must have planted them there. Now they're sure he didn't kill Shambless because he was in jail when the photographer Steve was killed by the same method. He's probably already back on the train by now. Don't think it was your fault. It wasn't. If I had seen Shambless threaten Juan, I would have told people too."

"I told them about Juan because I heard . . ."

"What? What did you hear, Michele? You can tell me."

"I heard my mother say something like, 'If nobody else kills that terrible man, I'm going to.' I was afraid somebody would think she did it."

"Oh, Michele, a lot of us wished he was dead. Nobody would ever suspect your mother of killing anybody."

Michele relaxed. "Of course, you're right, Gini. I was going nuts."

"Can't have my favorite dancer going nuts," I said.

Jonathan stood up. "Think I'll take Hawkeye for a walk down by the water. What time should I show up at the train?"

"We dance around ten, so come about nine-thirty and tell them I invited you. I'll make sure they save you and Hawkeye a good seat."

"Thanks, Gini," Jonathan said, walking toward the water with his left hand on Hawkeye's harness.

"Wait, Jonathan," Michele said. "Can I come with you?"

"Sure," he said, looking pleased. "I want to talk to you more about things that speak."

"My specialty," she said, catching up to him.

"See you later," he said to me. He and Michele and Hawkeye headed for the beach, with Hawkeye guiding Jonathan around trees and rocks. Michele hurried to keep up.

The waiter came out of the café to greet me in English. "*Hola,* señora. What would you like?"

"How did you know I speak English?" I asked.

"You look American," he said.

"How docs an American look?" I asked.

"As if the whole world is a gift. As if you want to find out everything about wherever you are. As if you belong anywhere you find yourself."

"Is that good? Sounds a little arrogant."

"Oh, it's very good," he said. "I wish I felt like that. Would you like some tea, señora? Or a vermouth?"

"Too early for vermouth. I'll take a tea. Thank you."

I wondered if that's true about Americans. Do we look as if we own the world? I leaned back in my chair, a white umbrella shielding me from the sun. I looked around at the houses perched on the hills, the little bridges crossing from one small island to another. How did I get to be so lucky? I have four good and dear friends, a man who loves me and I love him. I have the chance to see so much of this fascinating world filming documentaries. I get paid to do something as natural to me as taking pictures—dancing— with my best friends. Can't get much better than that.

I was totally content, my eyes closed to enjoy the warmth of the sun, when a high, thin voice said, "Could I talk to you?"

I opened my eyes. My peaceful day disappeared into the sea. Dora was standing next to me, bundled up in a sweater on this gorgeous day, shifting from foot to foot."

"Oh, please do," I said with all the enthusiasm of a condemned prisoner.

She sat down. In a voice I could barely hear, she said, "I want to apologize to you. I followed you down here when I saw you leave the train."

"You don't owe me an apology," I said. "You didn't do anything wrong."

"Oh, yes, I did," she said. "I was very rude to

you when you found my ring. I'm sorry. I was out of my mind when I lost that ring because of that picture of my daughter. I should have been grateful."

"Well, of course you were upset. I don't blame you. I'm glad I found it and was able to give it back to you. At first I didn't know it was yours, but then I remembered that you were wearing it in the restaurant. Even Shambless admired it. It's a lovely ring."

The waiter brought my tea and Dora asked for a cup too.

"I wanted to tell you more about my daughter," Dora said. "I wanted you to know why she was so precious to me."

"Tell me about her," I said, leaning toward her, no longer resentful of her presence.

"Well, as I told you before, she was born with cystic fibrosis. Do you know what that is?"

"I know it has something to do with the lungs."

"It's a disease that causes the lungs to clog. You have to clear them every day or the child will die. She was born with it. I don't have it, but I had a gene that carried it and so did her father. She spent so much of her life in the hospital. I had to learn how to clear her lungs when they filled up. She was such a brave little girl. She would never give up even when she was so sick. I worried every minute of her life that she would die that day."

"How long did you have her?"

"Until she was ten. And then one day I took her to the hospital. She never came home."

Dora's mouth trembled and her eyes filled with tears. She couldn't talk. I took her hand and held it in both of mine.

"I'm so sorry, Dora."

"Thank you," she said, pulling her hand away, reaching in her purse for a tissue. "That's why the ring is so important to me. It's my favorite picture of her. I guess that's why I was so impatient with you. I was afraid I'd lost it."

"How did your husband take all of this?" I asked.

She spat out the words. "He left us as soon as he found out that she was sick, that she would always be sick, that he would have to take care of her. He couldn't handle it. I have no idea where he is. I don't want to know."

My heart ached for this poor woman. What an incredibly sad life.

"Is that why you are such a fan of Shambless?" I asked. "Was he kind of a friend, even though you didn't really know him?"

She looked down at her lap, held the tissue to her nose. "I guess you could say that," she said. She looked at me. "Do you have any children?"

"No," I said. "But there's a little girl . . ." I wasn't sure whether Dora would be interested in my story about the little girl in India I wanted to adopt.

I was just going to let it go, but Dora said, "Tell me about her."

"Well, she's about eleven," I said. "I met her when I was filming a documentary about an orphanage in India. Her parents died of a disease and she was sent to the orphanage. The day I saw her for the first time she was reading about Jonah and the whale in the Bible. I started talking to her."

Dora leaned forward. "What's her name?" she asked.

"Amalia," I said. "She's so bright. I couldn't bear to think of her living out her life in that orphanage. It was clean and neat, but sterile, quiet. No laughing children running back and forth. No toys or swings or slides. Just well-behaved little robots, surviving. The nuns were all efficient, well-meaning, conscientious people, but they had no time to take a child on their laps to read to them or tell them a story or play with them. They did their jobs. You know what I mean, Dora?"

"Oh, yes," she said. "Poor little girl." She reached out to me but withdrew her hand almost immediately. I could see that this woman had a real problem touching people or being touched.

"She asked me if I would take her back to America with me," I said. "I told her I would do my best. I talked to the head of the orphanage, but it seems there are lots of rules about foreigners adopting children from India. The Indian government is not in favor of it. I haven't given up, though. I have some friends who are trying to help me adopt her. I want her so much."

"I hope you get her," Dora said. "Little girls are so sweet."

She took a sip of her tea and then stood up. "I won't bother you anymore," she said. "I'll get back to the train. I just wanted you to know that I didn't mean to be so rude."

I stood, too, and tried to put my arms around her, but she was stiff, unresponsive.

"It's all right, Dora. I understand. I'm so sorry about your daughter."

She almost smiled. "I'll see you later."

Watching her walk up the stairway to the station, I thought again how lucky I was. I settled back with my tea. The sun caressed me, the white buildings soothed me, the blue sea made me almost happy again.

My mind kept going back to my conversation with Dora. The picture of her sad-eyed little girl with the pale face in Dora's ring was still etched in my brain.

I wondered if I'd ever be able to adopt Amalia. Even though I didn't give birth to her, I thought of her as my child. I wanted to take her everywhere—to Paris and London and Rome. To Costa Rica and Rio. To Alaska and Hawaii and Japan. To

China and Thailand and Russia and Africa. I wanted her to see the whole world.

The sound of sandals clicking on the patio near me made me open my eyes. Geoffrey and Danielle were standing there.

"We're looking for our daughter," Geoffrey said. "We walked up to the chapel at the top of the hill and thought she was right behind us. We figured she must have come here to talk to you."

"She did," I said. "I always love talking to her."

"Where is she?" Danielle asked.

"She met this terrific guy and they're walking down by the beach. They should be back in a few minutes. Sit down and talk to me."

"What terrific guy?" Geoffrey asked.

"He works in Boston, has a guide dog, and Michele told him about a new talking device that attaches to a camera on your glasses that he hadn't heard about. She has a fascinating career. Very twenty-first century."

"We're so proud of her," Danielle said. "Although I have to admit I don't understand half the things she's talking about."

"I know what you mean," I said. "Geoffrey, what's happening with Julie? Are you going to represent her?"

"If they actually accuse her of anything, I will," he said. "Right now she's sort of in limbo. They don't have anything on her, but she's still under suspicion. There was no evidence she killed Steve."

"You were so good to help her. She's lucky you were on the train."

"She's still wary of me," he said. "I only volunteered because I was afraid they'd trick her into some kind of confession. I thought she needed legal advice, but I don't think she's convinced of that."

"What's she doing now?"

"She was going to pack her things and go back to America as soon as she could, but I think I persuaded her not to do that."

"Would Javier let her leave?" I asked.

"Probably not. She's still a witness, even if she didn't kill Steve, since she found his body. She'll have to testify at the trial if they ever figure out who did it."

"Who do you think did it?" I asked him.

"I'm pretty sure it was you, Gini," he said, grinning and backing away from my uppercut.

"There's our daughter now," Danielle said, waving to Michele as she ran after Jonathan and Hawkeye coming toward us.

"Gini, wait til you see what Hawkeye found," Michele said.

She kissed her mother and father, and handed me a small plastic bag full of what looked like tea leaves.

"Oh, Mom, Dad," she said, "this is Jonathan, and this amazing dog is Hawkeye."

Geoffrey and Danielle shook hands with Jonathan and patted Hawkeye.

"Where did you find this?" I asked.

"Hawkeye was sniffing around a tree down by the water," Jonathan said. "We kept tugging at him, but he wouldn't budge. He started to scratch the ground and kept digging until he came to this bag. When he found it, he jumped back, and sneezed, and pawed at the bag again. I was going to leave it there, but Michele said, 'Wait.' "

"Gini, I remembered what you said about them finding oleander leaves in Juan's room," Michele said. "I don't really know what oleander smells like, but this bag had such a strong, sweet smell, I thought I should bring it to you. Is that what oleander smells like? "

"I'm no expert either, Michele," I said, "but it's the same fragrance those oleander flowers at the restaurant had. I'm so glad you brought them to me. The same person who put the oleander leaves in Juan's room must have buried the rest of them under that tree down by the shore. As soon as we get back I'll give them to the inspector."

I patted the Lab again and gave him a hug. "Good boy, Hawkeye," I said. "You're a good detective." Then I remembered the rules about patting a guide dog.

"Is it okay to pet him now, Jonathan?" I asked.

"Sure," Jonathan said. "He deserves some extra hugs today, I think."

Just then, Rafaela appeared with some of the other passengers from the bus. "Are you hungry?" she asked. "We're headed for the Restaurante Villa Blanca for lunch. Want to come?"

"Lead on, Rafaela," I said. "The only thing I like better than dancing is eating."

Hawkeye gave my leg a nudge.

"Oh, Rafaela, is it all right if my friend Hawkeye and his friend Jonathan join us? They're not on the train, but I would really love to have them come with us."

"Of course," Rafaela said. She patted Hawkeye. "Come on, Hawkeye, and bring your friend along."

We followed her to a restaurant overlooking the ocean.

The owner welcomed us and conferred with Rafaela about the day's menu.

"You're in luck," Rafaela said. "The specialty today is one of their most famous dishes—*oricio*. That's sea urchin, stuffed with asparagus and caviar. It's unbelievably good. And there's *pitu de caleya*—chickens and fish. Or you can have suckling pig, rockfish, or any kind of shellfish. Everything is delicious, but I do recommend the *oricio*."

I joined Tina, who was sitting with Mark and Sam. "Where's the rest of us?" I asked her.

"Mike and Mary Louise weren't hungry. They're walking up to that little chapel on the hill," Tina said. "I don't know where Janice is. Pat just disappeared. The last time I saw her, she was in the dining car having a cup of coffee with Denise."

Tina and I can read each other's minds after all these years. We knew exactly where our friends were and whom they were with. I missed Alex a lot at that point. I knew Tina was thinking about Peter.

Seeing Mark reminded me that I had noticed him down by the rocks burying something. Should I ask him about it? What if it was oleander leaves? I had to know.

"Mark," I said. "I was taking some photos down by the water and I thought I saw you down there too."

"Yeah, that was me," he said. "I like to take a walk in the morning when everything is new and fresh."

"What were you burying in the sand?" I asked. "Should we look for another body?" I pretended to look around. "Let's see, who's missing?"

Mark looked embarrassed. "Somebody's dog had done his business right where everybody walks. I thought I'd bury it so no one would step in it."

"What a good guy you are," I said, relieved. "I never look where I'm walking when I'm taking pictures, so you probably saved me from stinky shoes. Thanks, Mark!"

"Any time, Gini. Can't have dancers with poop on their shoes."

"What are you guys eating?" I asked Mark. "As restaurateurs, what do you think of the food on this trip?"

"Next to France, this is the best," he said. "Especially the seafood. It's the freshest. They cook it simply and perfectly. We're collecting recipes as we go, but it's hard to get seafood this fresh in New York."

"This *oricio* tastes like they pulled it out of the ocean and ran into the kitchen to cook it before we could sit down," Sam said.

"Were you always interested in food and cooking and owning restaurants?" I asked.

"I was," Sam said. "From the time I was little, I loved reading magazines about food and restaurants. My mother was French and a fantastic cook. She could make the simplest foods taste like she had spent all day making them. They were delicate, multilayered flavors, melt-in-your mouth terrines and bourguignons. What I loved most about those pictures in magazines was the décor of the restaurants. I didn't call it décor then. I just loved the look of dining rooms that were quietly elegant with rugs on the floor, vaulted ceilings, hushed voices, white table cloths, flowers everywhere."

"It's hard to find a restaurant in New York like that anymore," I said. "Now it's all hardwood floors, bare ceilings, lots of noise and clattering, paper cloths on the tables. No sense of elegance. Why is that?"

"People want a place that's lively, with noise and bare floors, ceilings and tables," Sam said. "Our place is different, though."

"What's it like?" I asked.

"Well, for one thing, we have flowers everywhere. Small, elegant arrangements on the tables, huge vases full of flowers on every other surface. We've soundproofed the ceiling and put thick rugs on the floor. We don't crowd the tables against each other. There's room to breathe and talk without hearing every word at the next table."

"I'm bringing Alex there as soon as we get back home," I told him.

"We'll give you one of the best meals you've ever had," Mark said, taking a mouthful of the *oricio*. "Except possibly for this one. Wait until you try this, Gini. It's perfection."

It *was* perfection. I was enjoying every bit of this superb lunch when I noticed Dora a few tables over with the young boy in the wheelchair and his mother. She looked up and studied me for a minute. I waved at her.

"Are you best friends with Shambless's biggest fan now, Gini?" Mark asked, looking over at Dora.

"Not exactly, but we talked at the café this morning," I said. "She told me about her little girl who died of cystic fibrosis." I looked over at Dora again. "I feel so sorry for her."

"That's a terrible illness," Mark said.

Dora watched us briefly and then left the restaurant.

Javier and Janice joined us at our table.

"So what's happening, you two?" Tina asked.

"Haven't seen you around much," I said.

"Javier's been working," Janice said. "He just came back to the train to bring me to this restaurant."

"I see you're having the *oricio*," he said to us. "Great choice. How do you like it?"

We made happy sounds about our main course. Javier ordered the same thing from the owner. He poured a glass of wine for Janice and raised it to her before drinking. His phone vibrated and he excused himself from the table. After a short conversation he returned.

"I am so sorry to have to leave you, but there was news from headquarters in Ribadeo. They have released Juan and he will be rejoining the train. There was not enough evidence to hold him."

"What about the poison in his room?" I asked.

"It looks like somebody planted it there to make it look like he was the murderer. It was the same oleander poison that killed both Shambless and Steve. Anyway, I have to go back to the train and make sure he's all right. I'll see you tonight at the performance."

"Wait, Javier," I said. "I have something to give you." I handed him the bag of oleander leaves.

"Where did you get this?" he asked.

"See that golden Lab over there with my friend Jonathan? He dug this up by one of the trees down by the water. They're oleander leaves, aren't they?"

"This is very important, Gini. The lab will do tests on this bag and it should tell us who it belonged too. Good work."

"You should thank Hawkeye," I said. "He wouldn't leave that tree until he dug this up."

Javier walked over to Jonathan, introduced himself, and leaned down to pat Hawkeye. "Give him anything he wants to eat—it's on me," Javier said.

As he started to leave, Janice said to him, "Can I come back with you?"

"It's something I have to do alone, Janice," Javier said. "I'll see you soon."

When he was gone, I looked at Janice. "Are you okay, hon?"

"I guess so, Gini. I'm not sure. He shuts me out of the important parts of his life."

"After all, Janice," Mark said, "he's a police inspector. Some things have to remain confidential."

"I know that, Mark, but I want to be with him all the time."

"Are you in love with him, Jan?" Tina asked.

"Not really," she said. "I love being with him, but I don't see much future for us. I'm not going to live in Spain, and he's not going to live in America." She looked resigned. "I'm just taking it one day at a time and enjoying every minute with him. He's so confident, so sure of himself, so in charge. It's hard to meet a man like that in America."

"I agree," Mark said. "Most people at home seem isolated, depending more and more on their iPads and smartphones. They don't seem to be aware of other people or the world anymore."

"Sometimes I think the art of conversation is dying out altogether," Tina said.

"Let's bring it back," I said.

I was too full for dessert. I waved good-bye to my friends and started back to the train. As I was climbing the steps leading to the platform, I heard voices calling to me.

"Gini. Wait up."

I turned around and saw Mary Louise and Mike running to catch up to me.

"You missed a great lunch," I told them. "Something called *oricio*. You should have been there. Where were you anyway?"

"We went to that little chapel up on the hill," Mary Louise said. "It was so lovely. So quiet. We decided to stay there instead of going to the restaurant. We talked . . . And in that holy place we decided . . ."

"What?" I was worried. "What did you decide?"

"That we want to be together," Mike said.

"What do you mean, 'you want to be together'?" I asked. "You don't mean . . ."

"Yes, we do, Gini," Mary Louise said. "I'm going to divorce George. Mike and I are going to get married."

I gathered up every bit of strength I had to stay calm, to talk quietly, not to yell, "Are you crazy?"

Instead, I managed to say, "You've only known each other three days. Oh, honey, just wait until we get back home before you decide this. At least give George a chance."

"I have given George a chance," Mary Louise said. "For twenty years. That's long enough. I know I love Mike and I want to be with him."

I didn't trust myself to say anything else. We walked back to the train in silence.

Chapter 12

What Delicious Tea!

As I passed Dora's room, her door opened and there she stood wearing yet another gray outfit—this time, a T-shirt and sweatpants. With a stiff smile, she said, "Could you come in for a cup of tea, Gini? I want to show you some pictures of Darlene."

I couldn't think of any reason not to, so I said, "Sure, I have a few minutes."

She had put several pictures on the table in her suite. There was a tray with a teapot and cookies on the dresser top.

She poured a cup of tea and handed it to me. I took a sip. There was something odd about it.

A strong, flowery fragrance and very sweet taste. It was the same strong smell that came from the bag that Hawkeye found down by the shore. Oleander leaves. I put the cup back in its saucer so quickly some of it spilled on the table. I looked at Dora. She was watching me intently.

"What an interesting flavor, Dora," I said. "Don't think I've ever had it before. What kind is it?"

"It's my own blend," she said, pushing my cup closer to me and mopping up the tea that had spilled with her napkin. "I make it at home and always carry it with me. I like it better than the kind they give you in restaurants. Here, have a cookie."

I shook my head. "No, thanks," I said. "I don't like to eat too much before we dance. Aren't you having any tea?"

"Oh, yes, I'll have some in a minute," she said, putting the pictures in front of me.

"This is Darlene when she was born." Her face contorted in pain, she showed me a picture of a man holding a baby.

"Here she is with her father. It's the only one I have of him with her. I only keep it because she's in the picture with him."

The photo showed a balding, lean-faced man holding his baby daughter as if he wanted to get rid of her as soon as possible. He was scowling and not looking into the camera.

"How did you meet him?" I asked.

"I was a secretary in a firm of accountants where he worked. We used to go out for drinks. He seemed nice enough. Anyway, I married him. He was never a lot of laughs, but he worked hard. I stayed home after I got pregnant with Darlene."

She started to pour a cup of tea, but stopped, her face grim. "He wasn't exactly thrilled that I was going to have a baby. He said it would be all right if I had a boy. I tried to tell him that it might be a girl, but he said he wanted a son."

"What happened when you had a girl and she was diagnosed with cystic fibrosis?" I asked.

"He couldn't handle it at all. He kept saying it had to come from my side because all his relatives were healthy. I tried to tell him that the doctor said it was caused by a gene on both sides—from the mother and the father. He would curse and yell at me when I told him that. Finally he got so abusive and cruel that I told him to leave. He just disappeared. I've never heard from him again to this day. He never sent a penny to care for her or for me."

"What did you live on?"

"Food stamps. Disability money. I don't need a lot of money where I live. That's how I could save enough for this trip. The benefits would all have stopped when she was eighteen. I don't know what I would have done then. She died before I had to deal with that. I didn't want her to die. I loved her. I miss her." She wiped away a tear.

"Watching Shambless must have been a comfort to you through all of this," I said. I don't know what made me say that.

She was very still. Her head was down. When she raised it, there was a look of such fierce hatred on her face that I felt like I'd been slapped.

"He wasn't a comfort, he was the devil. I hated him. He was always disparaging people with a disability. He would say things like, 'They should all be put out of their misery. They have terrible lives. They ruin the families they were born into. Every doctor should be allowed to get rid of them in the delivery room.' He went on and on about people like me who live on government money. He said we were all freeloaders and should work for our money or get it from our families."

She stopped, her face a mask. "I was taking care of my little girl, running back and forth to the hospital trying to keep her alive, living on practically no money, and this monster was telling me my daughter and I should be eliminated."

"You seemed to admire him so much in the restaurant and on the bus," I said, with a great deal of effort not to show my shock. "We all thought you were a real fan."

She smiled. It was a smile of such vindictiveness and hatred that I knew she had killed him.

"That's what I wanted everyone to think." She stopped and picked up my teacup. "You're not drinking your tea. Let me warm it up for you."

She picked up the teapot and poured another few drops into my cup and handed it to me.

"Oh, Dora," I said, standing up. "I wish I could stay, but I've got to get ready to dance. There's so little room in the suites, we have to change in shifts." I edged my way toward the door, talking fast, desperate to get out of there. "Hope you're coming to see us tonight."

She grabbed my arm. "Stay a little longer," she said, her eyes manic. "You haven't finished your tea. I want to tell you more about Darlene."

"I'd love to hear about her, Dora," I said, tugging at the door, which was locked. "We'll get together soon and talk some more, I promise."

I wrenched my arm away from her, unlocked the door, and swung it open.

She reached out for me again, but I managed to get through the door and out into the hall. I looked back. I could see her face, a mask of anger and venom glaring at me from her suite.

My knees were wobbly as I opened the door to our room.

Tina took one look at me and guided me to the bed.

"Gini, what is it?" she said. "You look terrible. What's the matter?"

I told her what had happened.

"What makes you think she killed Shambless?" she asked. "Was it just the tea?"

"The tea and her face as she talked about her daughter and her husband and how much she hated Shambless. Tina, she just sounded crazier and crazier. Of course, I have no proof that she killed him, but I wasn't going to stick around and drink any more of that tea. It really tasted weird."

"You have to tell the inspector," Tina said. "I mean it, Gini. Go and find him and tell him now."

"What am I going to tell him?" I said. "She didn't actually do anything to me. I can't accuse her of murder because her tea tasted funny. She didn't confess to killing Shambless. She just said he was a terrible man. That doesn't prove anything."

"I know, Gini," Tina said. "But she seems to think you know she killed him. She might try to kill you again. Next time she might succeed. Please, please, tell the inspector. Let him decide if she's guilty or not."

"You're right," I said. "I don't even know where he is."

"In the restaurant he said he was coming back to the train to see if Juan is all right. Try the bar."

I don't know why I ever argue with Tina. She's always right. I left our suite and headed toward the bar.

By the time I got there, I was still arguing with myself as to whether to tell Javier what had happened. What proof did I have, after all?

No, Tina was right. I had to tell someone. Dora might come after me again. I couldn't figure out why she thought I was a threat to her. I hadn't done anything to make her think that. Best to let the inspector sort it out.

Javier and Juan were talking when I walked into the lounge. They didn't notice me until I was right next to Javier.

"Señora Miller," he said. "How nice to see you. To what do I owe this pleasure?"

"Inspector," I said. I didn't know how to start. How could I tell him that I thought Dora was trying to kill me because her tea smelled funny?

"Sit down, Gini," he said. "You look as if you have something to tell me. What is it?"

His face was concerned, kind. Maybe I had misjudged him all this time. Maybe he wouldn't think I was some kind of nutcase.

"Inspector. Javier. Something just happened that I think I should tell you about. I know it sounds really weird, but I think Dora Lindquist just tried to poison me."

His face was instantly serious, attentive. "What happened?" he asked.

"Well." I stopped. How could I put this so he wouldn't think I was imagining this whole thing?

I dove in. "About a half hour ago, Dora invited me into her suite for some tea. She said she wanted to show me pictures of her daughter. You know, the one who died. I thought, 'Why not?' Up until then I believed that she was a devoted fan of Shambless. I mean, she talked about him as if he were a god."

"So you accepted her invitation and . . ." the inspector urged.

"She had a whole bunch of photographs of her daughter. She told me about her husband who deserted her when he found out their little girl had cystic fibrosis. She poured me a cup of tea."

"And?" He seemed to be growing impatient.

"I was feeling sorry for her. I took a sip of the tea and was almost bowled over by the strong scent and very sweet flavor of the tea."

"What kind was it?"

"She said it was a blend she made herself and always carried with her. She seemed a little too eager for me to try it. I took one sip, and I knew it was oleander that I smelled because of that bag of leaves I gave you this morning. The one that Hawkeye found. The tea smelled just like that. I decided not to drink any more of it."

"Good choice," Javier said.

"The weird thing, Javier," I said, "was that when I mentioned Shambless, she said she hated him. You should have seen her face. It was distorted with rage when she talked about him. She said he was always saying bad things about children with disabilities. How doctors should get rid of them in the delivery room. How parents got all that government money to take care of children who shouldn't be allowed to live. I nearly fell off my chair, because up until then, I thought she worshipped him."

"That still doesn't explain why she would want to harm you, though," Javier said.

"For some reason she thinks I know that she killed Shambless. I don't know why, but I'm sure she was trying to poison me with that tea."

Javier grabbed my arm. "Come on, Gini. I want to have a taste of that tea."

"You don't think I'm nuts?" I said.

"Maybe, but you've told me enough so that I want to find out more," he said. "Let's go."

He hurried me along the corridor to Dora's suite and knocked on her door. There was no answer.

Javier knocked again, louder. "Open the door, please, Señora Lindquist. It's Inspector Cruz."

The door opened. Dora's weak smile turned to a look of hostility when she saw that I was with the inspector.

"We'd like to talk to you for a minute, señora," Javier said.

"Of course, Inspector. Please come in."

We walked into her suite. The photos of her daughter were still lined up on the dresser. All signs of our tea party had disappeared. There was no pitcher of tea, no plate of cookies, no cups and saucers. The only remainder of my visit to her was a strong, sweet smell in the air. The same smell that kept me from drinking the tea she offered me.

"What can I do for you, Inspector," Dora said.

"Señora Miller said you invited her in for tea

and to see pictures of your daughter. Is that true?"

"Yes, of course. Señora Miller had expressed some interest in hearing more about Darlene. I got out some photos for her to see. I offered her a cup of tea. I always do that. It's a Southern custom," she said.

"Do you have any tea left?" the inspector asked. "I always enjoy a cup of tea in the afternoon."

"I would be happy to make a fresh pot of tea for you, Inspector," she said. "I don't have any of the tea I shared with Señora Miller. She didn't seem to care for it anyway."

"Don't bother," the inspector said. "I wonder if I might see the teapot and teacups you used."

"Certainly, Inspector."

Dora opened the door of a small cabinet under the table by the window and pulled out the flowered teapot and two cups and saucers I had seen before. They were sparkling clean. There couldn't have been one whisper of tea left in any of them.

The inspector turned to me.

"Señora Miller, is this the teapot and cups Señora Lindquist served you from?"

Dora was watching me intently.

"They're the ones, Inspector."

"Would you mind showing me the tea you served to Señora Miller?" the inspector asked.

Dora reached in the cabinet again and pulled out a bag of tea leaves. The label on the bag said ROSE HIP TEA.

"Is this the only kind of tea you have, Señora Lindquist?"

"Yes, this is my favorite kind. It's a little sweet for some people's taste. I guess for Señora Miller it was way too sweet."

Dora drew herself up and pursed her lips.

"May I ask, Inspector, why you're interested in my choice of tea?"

"Señora Miller thought perhaps you were serving her your own special brand of tea."

"Oh, I see." Dora said, glaring at me. "I have been quite aware for some time, Inspector, that Ms. Miller suspects me of killing Mr. Shambless. I certainly don't know where she got that idea. I don't have any oleander tea, if that's what she told you."

"Señora Miller was under the impression that you did not like Mr. Shambless as much as you insisted you did," the inspector continued. "She claims you said you hated him because of his comments about children with disabilities."

Dora looked the inspector right in the eye. "I said no such thing. I admired Mr. Shambless. I was devastated when he was murdered. She's the one who was heard to say she would like to kill him. You should be looking for poison in her room, Inspector."

"I'm sorry to have disturbed you, señora," the inspector said. "We have to follow up all leads, you understand."

"I do understand, Inspector," she said. "Next time, I hope you have a more credible witness than someone who obviously dislikes me because of my conservative beliefs."

She opened the door of her suite and stood there waiting for us to leave.

As I followed the inspector out into the corridor, Dora said to me in a low voice, "I'll be in touch with you soon, hoofer."

It was not a friendly good-bye.

Javier walked me back to my suite. He didn't say anything.

"She lied, you know, Inspector," I said, not at all sure he would believe me.

He surprised me. "I know that. You have no reason to make any of this up, Gini," he said. "Of course I believe you. But we have a problem. A suspect without any evidence. I suppose rose hip tea would have as sweet a taste and smell as oleander. It's what you told me she said about Shambless after pretending all along that she thought he was God that convinced me you are telling the truth."

"Javier, how come you believe me instead of Dora?" I asked.

"Because you're a friend of Janice," he said. "She wouldn't have a liar for a friend."

"Thank you for that," I said. "What will you do now?"

"I'm afraid there's nothing I can do until she makes her next move." He frowned. "Unfortunately, that next move might be against you."

He took my hand in both of his. It was ice cold. "I'm responsible for the health of all dancers on this train," he said. "Don't worry. I'll make sure nothing happens to you."

"Thanks, Javier," I said.

"Are you dancing tonight?" he asked me.

"Yes, if my legs hold up. They're a bit shaky at the moment."

"Well, she can't kill you while you're dancing."

"Are you sure?"

"Reasonably." He smiled. "I'll be here. Don't worry."

Tina was waiting for me. "What happened? Tell me."

I told her about our visit to Dora and the rose hip tea.

Tina made me sit down on my bed. "Listen, Gini, we don't have to dance tonight, you know. I'll just tell Eduardo that we can't do it."

Her kindness brought tears to my eyes. "I'll be all right, Tina. As Javier said, she can't kill me when I'm dancing."

"We have a little while before the performance. Rafaela is giving a Spanish lesson. I think I'll go. Want to come? It might get your mind off Dora for a while."

"Sounds like a good plan," I said. "I'll join you."

Chapter 13

Hablas Español?

Rafaela stood by a blackboard at the front of the car. The room was small and lined with bookshelves. It was a library and a place to play Scrabble and other board games most of the time.

"I want to teach you some basic phrases in Spanish," she said. "Some things that might be useful if you come back to our country again. I hope you will."

The next time I come back to this country, I thought, I want to visit some peaceful little village where nobody has killed anybody for a long, long time.

"The most basic phrase you might want to use," Rafaela said, "is 'Hello, my name is . . .' This is how it's written: *Hola. Me llamo . . .* I am called . . . It's pronounced 'may yamo' . . . Let's go around the room and you can each tell me your name."

We all told her our names and she smiled. *"Muy bien,"* she said. She pronounced it "mooey bee-en," which most of us already knew meant "very good."

"You might want to ask the other person his or her name," Rafaela said. "You would say, *'¿Como se llama usted?'* Try that. Ask your neighbor her name and tell her yours."

We all exchanged names with each other and, of course, smart aleck wise ass that I am, I couldn't resist asking Rafaela how to say "I forgot my name."

She laughed, and said, "You would say, *'Me olvide,'* but it's not the best way to make friends in Spain."

A woman in the back raised her hand. "Rafaela, how do you ask where the restroom is?"

"Good question," Rafaela answered. "The best way to ask is *'¿Donde estan los servicios, por favor?'* If you ask, *'¿Donde estan el bano?'* you are asking for a room with a bathtub in it. You don't really need a bath."

"How do you say, 'Where is a good restaurant?'" Mary Louise asked.

"Do you ever think of anything besides food?" I asked her.

"Occasionally," she said, "but the food here is so good I want to be able to ask if I'm here by myself some someday."

"Easy," Rafaela said. "You just ask, '*¿Donde puedo encontrar un restaurante bueno?*' You've probably figured out that *donde* means 'where,' so just say '*¿Donde esta . . .*'and look up what you want to find in your Spanish-English dictionary. Let's try something a little more difficult. Give me an example of something you want to say."

"How about 'Are you married?' " Janice asked, and we all laughed.

"You would say, '*¿Esta usted casado?*' That's if you're talking to a man. I see one gentleman here. He would say, '*¿Esta usted casada?*' "

"I don't think my wife would like that," he said, pointing to the woman sitting next to him. She laughed along with him.

Rafaela said, "What else?"

Pat said, "How about, 'I think you need to see a good therapist.' "

"Again," Rafaela said, "That's that's probably not the best way to make friends in Spain, but if you meet somebody really disturbed, you would say, '*Creo que se necesita un buen terapeuta cognitivo.*' "

"What's the best travel tip you would give someone planning a vacation in Spain?" Tina asked.

"Always working," I said to her.

"Well, who knows better than Rafaela?" she said.

"Gracias," Rafaela said. "I'm sure you all know by now that means 'thank you.' But to answer Tina's question, I think the best travel tip is, if you don't know how to ask for something in Spanish, just smile and ask in English. You'll find most people here speak your language, or at least know enough to help you find what you want. Gini, we haven't heard from you. What would you like to say in Spanish?"

"Where is the nearest policeman?" I said.

"Do you really think you're going to need a policeman on this trip?" Rafaela asked.

"I sincerely hope not," I said. "But I'd just like to be prepared."

"Let's hope you will never need it, but if you do, the Spanish word for policeman is *'policia.'* "

She gazed around the car, and said, "You might want to take a class in Spanish when you get home. There are lots of online classes available. I'm prejudiced, I know, but I think it's a beautiful language."

We all applauded and left, saying *"gracias"* as we went out the door.

That night, after a light supper of cold shrimp and salad, I changed into my flapper clothes. Short filmy dress. Sexy garters. Silk headband across my forehead. Long string of beads swaying as I did a quick time step to get in the mood. Rosy knees and rhinestone earrings. I was psyched.

The audience was getting settled, talking and moving chairs, rustling, laughing, quieting down as Eduardo walked out on the dance floor.

"Ladies and gentlemen, I have the great pleasure of presenting our five Happy Hoofers, our beautiful flappers who will dance 'Forty-Second Street' for you."

The audience broke into wild applause as the CD started playing through the train's sound system. We tapped onto the stage, our flapper skirts flipping around our rouged knees, our rhinestone garters flashing as we swung into a time step. We shuffled off to Buffalo, did a few high kicks, then danced and swirled across the tiny stage. Could we be any sexier with our sensational legs, curvy bodies, and younger than young spirits? I can't help it. We were just the best. All of us dancing our hearts out, moving to that music as if it were written just for us.

The music switched to the Charleston. Instantly we were all flashing feet and bending knees. We were heating up this paneled railroad car, opening up the narrow gauge, flashing our smiles, flipping our curls, making that room sing, baby. We were the cat's meow, the top of the hill, the best of the best. We finished with a fast and sexy dance around the audience and back to the stage for our final bow.

Great roars of "hooray" and "more, more, more, formidable," and applause loud enough to reach the Picos de Europa mountains outside our train. We were flushed and laughing, being hugged by people we didn't know.

I saw Janice looking out across the audience, waiting for Javier, wondering where he was, but knowing that his work came first.

I started toward her to cheer her up. Before I could get to her, Tom pushed his way through the crowd around us and whispered something in her ear. She looked startled and then took his hand and followed him out of the car. Sylvia was nowhere in sight.

"Let's change and get something to eat," Tina said. "I don't know why, but I'm hungry all the time."

"Probably pregnant," I said.

"Bite your tongue," Tina said. "It would have to be another immaculate conception if I am. Oh, Gini, look, there's that great-looking Lab that was at the restaurant with us. He brought Jonathan with him. Fascinating guy."

"Oh, good," I said. "That's Hawkeye, the hero of the day."

We worked our way through the crowd.

"Hey there, Jonathan," I said when we reached him. "I'm glad you got here. Were you here for our dance?"

"Gini?" he said. "Is that you? I loved your 'Forty-Second Street.' It's one of my favorites."

"Jonathan, I'm with Tina. You met her at the restaurant."

"Hello, Jonathan," Tina said, shaking Jonathan's hand. "Okay if I pet Hawkeye?"

"Can we go somewhere where we can sit down? Then it's okay to pet him. He won't be working."

We walked over to the bar to get a *cava* from Juan. I was relieved to see him back behind the bar, unsmiling and stoic as usual.

"Juan, I'm so glad you're back," I said.

"I'm very glad to be back, señora."

"We all knew you couldn't have killed Shambless."

He didn't say anything, just looked at me as if to say, Then what was I doing in jail?

He handed us our *cavas* and we took them to a table on the side.

Tina reached down to pet Hawkeye when we were settled.

"Could I ask you a question?" she said to Jonathan.

"Sure," Jonathan said.

"I'm doing research for an article on guide dogs for *The Times* magazine. Could I talk to you about them when we get back home?"

"My favorite subject," Jonathan said. "I thought you worked for a bridal magazine."

"I do, but I also freelance when I can. Are you based in New York?"

"No, I'm in Boston," Jonathan said. "But I'd love to tell you about these dogs. They're amazing animals. The training is intense. Can you come up to Boston when we get back? I can put you in touch with some people who know a lot more about them than I do."

"That would be great. Thanks."

"I feel funny bringing this up," Jonathan said, "but it's hard to tell there was a murder on this train."

"Two, actually," Tina said.

"Well, how come it's party time," Jonathan said. "How come nobody is talking about it? Did they arrest the murderer? Do they know who buried the oleander leaves, or whatever they are, under that tree."

"No," I said. "I think I know who did it, but I don't have any evidence."

I looked around the room to be sure Dora wasn't listening to me, and continued in a lowered voice.

I told Jonathan about my tea party with Dora and my unfruitful visit to her afterward with the inspector.

"Wait a minute," Jonathan said. "You're basing your whole theory that Dora killed Shambless on her tea being too sweet?"

When he put it like that, it did sound a little weird. Was I just making this whole thing up about Dora because she made tea that smelled like oleanders?

No. My instincts were right. The look of hatred on her face when she talked about Shambless was real.

"I guess it sounds a little, uh, weak," I said. "But I know I'm right. Jonathan, her tea smelled exactly like that bag of leaves Hawkeye found. Even the inspector believed me. He told me to be careful. He thinks Dora will try to harm me again."

"Why are you still on this train?" Jonathan asked. "If I thought someone was trying to kill me, I'd be on the first plane home."

"Good question," I said. "I must be crazy."

"Why does she think you know that she's the killer?"

"Because I wouldn't drink the tea."

"But why would she try to give you poisoned tea in the first place?" Jonathan asked.

"I don't know. I think it's something to do with my finding the ring and returning it to her. She went bananas when she found out that I had opened the ring and seen the picture of her daughter. She yelled at me that I had no business opening the ring."

"Why?" Jonathan asked.

"The only thing I can think of is that there was something else inside that ring that she didn't want me to know about."

"Like?"

Then I got it. Of course. The reason she didn't want me to look inside her ring was that there was some residue of oleander powder inside. I remember thinking the picture was dusty. She must have opened her ring and emptied the poison into Shambless's wine at the restaurant when he was signing her menu. Why didn't I think of that before? Steve must have taken some footage of her with Shambless while he was filming the documentary. Maybe the film showed Dora putting the poison into his wine. She couldn't take a chance, so she stole his camera and then killed him too. That's it!

"Jonathan!" I said. "I've got it. I know how she killed Shambless and Steve, and why she's trying to kill me. I've got to find the inspector and tell him."

"Gini, are you sure?" Tina asked.

"Positive. I don't have time to tell you the whole thing now, but I've got to find the inspector. Sorry to rush off, Jonathan, but I gotta go."

I heard Tina say to Jonathan as I rushed off, "That's our Gini. When she gets an idea, she acts."

I found Eduardo talking to some of the passengers near the bar. I ran up to him.

"Eduardo," I said. "I have to find the inspector. Now. Do you know where he is?"

"He went back to headquarters in Ribadeo," Eduardo said. "Some kind of emergency at home. I don't think he'll be back until tomorrow. What is it, Señora Miller? Can I help you with something?"

"I don't think so, Eduardo," I said. "I really need to talk to the inspector."

Before I saw her, I felt Dora's eyes boring into me. She was talking to some people a few yards away. I knew she had heard what I said.

"Do you want to call him?" Eduardo asked. "Use my phone."

"Thanks, Eduardo, I think I'll go back to my suite and call him."

I ran back to the room and called the number Javier had given me.

There was no answer. It was late. The inspector must not be answering his phone. I left him a message to call me as soon as possible. "It's urgent," I said.

Gini's photography tip: Don't e-mail pictures of yourself in your underwear to anybody— they could end up on the news.

Chapter 14

Champagne In The Morning

I was fast asleep the next morning when Carlos knocked on our door. I made some kind of noise that sounded like, "Yes. Who is it?

"Restrictions have been lifted, señora," Carlos said. "The tour of Oviedo leaves in an hour," Carlos said. "I thought you might want to get something to eat before you go."

I muttered something that was an approximation of "Thank you, Carlos."

Tina had already left for breakfast, letting me sleep.

I had forgotten all about Oviedo. I picked up a copy of the day's schedule that Tina had put at the foot of my bed. "Visit to Oviedo in the morning to see cathedral and pre-Romanesque monuments on the Naranco Hill. Lunch at Restaurante El Raitán. Visit to cave in Covadonga in the afternoon." Sounded like a busy day. I thought of the photo ops I'd be missing if I didn't go.

I sat up, stretched, rubbed my eyes, and jumped into the shower.

An hour later, dressed, coffeed, and fed, I showed up at the tour bus where most of the passengers were already seated. I looked around for Javier, but he was nowhere in sight. As I climbed on the bus, I froze. Dora was sitting in the first row. She didn't say anything to me, but her face was hard and menacing. I moved to a seat farther back next to Tina.

I whispered to her as we sat down. "She scares me."

"Don't worry," she said. "Nothing can happen to you with all of us around you."

I relaxed. She was right. What could Dora do anyway? She couldn't force me to drink tea on the bus.

The coach started up and Rafaela spoke into her microphone. "Let me tell you a little bit about Oviedo. It's a really interesting place. I want to fill you in on its history."

We all quieted down to listen. Rafaela always had good things to tell us.

"Oviedo was originally a small city built around a Benedictine monastery in the eighth century by Fruela the First," she said. "The Muslims destroyed it and Fruela's son, Alfonso the Chaste, rebuilt the town."

"Sounds like a fun guy," Sam said, winning a laugh.

Rafaela soldiered on. "His successor, Ramiro, built a summer palace on Monte Naranco in the ninth century. We're going to see that today. It's amazing. What was called the audience chamber still remains and is now the Church of Saint María. There is no steeple. It's a perfect example of pre-Romanesque architecture—a total contrast to the superb Gothic cathedral built in the town in the fourteenth century, which you will also see. There is a plaza and a lovely town with some shops you might want to investigate. Best of all is the El Raitán restaurant where we'll go for lunch so you can enjoy the superb cuisine of Asturias—lots of hearty bean stews and marvelous apple cider."

Cheers went up from all sides of the bus. Rafaela laughed, "True art lovers, all of you heathens."

The coach stopped in front of the cathedral in the center of Oviedo. "Go explore on your own," Rafaela said. "Meet me back here at noon for lunch. After that, we'll go to Covadonga."

I entered the cathedral, which was breathtaking and elaborately Gothic, with magnificent rose windows and an altar carved with scenes from the life of Christ. Each of the small chapels on either side of the church held sculptures of saints. In one, there were statues of twelve musicians. The tombs of the kings of Asturias were in these chapels. We gasped at a Cross of the Angels made of wood, studded with jewels, a golden Cross of Victory with precious stones, and a silver-plated casket.

I walked down the main aisle of the cathedral and looked at the figures of Christ carved into the altarpiece. The morning light shone through the tall windows onto the altar. I felt totally at peace.

Outside, I took out my camera and took shots of the cathedral from all sides. I was photographing the carvings on the door, when it opened and Mark and Sam came out.

"Getting some good shots, Gini?" Mark asked.

"I could spend the whole morning taking pictures of this cathedral," I said. "The lighting is different on every side."

"Why don't you come with us to the Naranco Hill monument?" Mark asked. "We have something special in mind. We want you to take some pictures for us."

"Isn't it like two miles up there?" I asked.

"Yes, but you'll love it," Sam said. "You'll especially appreciate what will happen there."

"Give me a hint, Sam," I said.

"I can't," he said. "We want it to be a surprise. Please come with us. How often do you get to see something built in the ninth century?"

"Not much in New Jersey," I said, and slung my camera bag over my shoulder and followed them up the road to Naranco Hill.

After our two-mile hike with lots of stops to sit down, we reached what is now called the church of Santa María del Naranco. It's made of sandstone and marble and is a soft beigy color. There was no steeple. There were three arches in the middle of the building, separated by columns. The lower level was a crypt. To get to the main church on the upper level, we had to climb up a stone stairway on the outside of what was Ramiro's summer hunting lodge back in 848.

The inside of Santa María was decorated elaborately with medallions of birds, grapes, weird animals, and a Greek cross, which was the emblem of the Asturias monarchy. There was goldwork everywhere, sculptures, a fascinating combination of pre-Romanesque, ninth-century architecture with fourteenth-century Christian religious symbols.

I was admiring the carving on the altar, when Mark said to me, "Gini, would you be our witness?"

"What do you mean?" I asked.

"We were going to get married when we got back to New York," Mark said, "but we thought it would be really meaningful to exchange vows here in this building that started out a palace and now is a church. It suits our sense of the strangeness of life." He looked at Sam. "You sure you want to do this? It probably is more a marriage here than back home."

Sam looked at his partner with a love that I could feel in my own heart.

"There will never be anyone else for me but you, Mark. You know that," Sam said.

"I'd be thrilled to be your witness," I told them, my voice choked up.

Mark and Sam stood facing each other in this holy place, the light streaming through the windows as if it were blessing them.

"Do you, Sam Thompson, light of my life, take me to be your lawfully wedded husband?"

I could see the tears in Sam's eyes as he said, "I do." He continued, his voice full of emotion, "Do you, Mark Fuller, my dearest friend, take me to be your lawfully wedded partner?"

"With all my heart," he said. The two men kissed in this ninth-century church in the middle of Oviedo, Spain.

"I'm not sure you're allowed to kiss in a cathedral unless you're getting married," Geoffrey said, coming up behind us with Danielle.

"Oh, but we are getting married, Geoffrey," Mark said. "Sam and I just exchanged vows. You and Danielle and Gini are the first to know."

"Congratulations, you two," Danielle said, embracing each one. "We have to celebrate," she said. "Geoffrey, let's take them to that café in the plaza and celebrate with champagne."

"Danielle, it's only ten-thirty in the morning," I said.

"I know," she said, "but tea won't do it. Come on. We're in Spain, not New Jersey."

"Let's go for it," Mark said.

We left the church. Outside in the warm air of northern Spain, I cherished the thought of these two friends who sanctified their love on this day.

We found a little café in the middle of the square, and Geoffrey ordered the most expensive bottle of champagne they had. We were raising our glasses in a toast to love, Spain, and whatever happens next, when our friends descended upon us, all talking at once.

"Champagne in the middle of the morning? What's going on here?" Tina asked. "And where's my glass?"

"Gini, what's happening?" Pat asked.

"We're celebrating Mark and Sam's exchange of vows in the church up on the hill."

"Is drinking in the morning the custom in Spain?" Mary Louise said. "If it is, I'm all for it."

Geoffrey ordered several more bottles. When everyone had a glass of champagne, he said, "Here's to Mark and Sam, who have joined hearts and souls with each other for life, and to whom I wish the same happiness Danielle and I have enjoyed for the last twenty years."

"God bless you both," Danielle said, raising her glass.

My friends all talked at once.

"Is it legal?" said Pat, our voice of reason, sipping on a glass of sparkling water.

"For us, it is," Mark said. "But when we get home, we'll make it legal in the state of New York."

"To the state of New York," Pat said. "And to your happiness forever and ever."

Little by little our group grew. Denise ran up to toast us. Tom congratulated his friends and shared a glass of champagne with Janice.

"Where's Sylvia?" she asked him.

"She's shopping in one of those little stores," he said. "Where's Javier?"

"I don't know," she said. "I thought he would join us on this trip, but something must have come up. Cheers, Tom."

"Cheers, Jan," he said, clearly happy to be with her.

Rafaela, wondering where her American tourists had disappeared to, found us drinking and celebrating.

We told her about Mark and Sam's exchange of vows in the church and she was thrilled. "This has never happened to me before," she said. "I am so happy for you. Are you willing to continue this wedding reception at our restaurant, El Raitán? I know the owner will want to prepare something special for you. Everything there is good, but he'll want to make something just for you. Bring the drinks with you."

All of us slightly tipsy—except Pat, of course—raised our glasses one more time. We followed Rafaela to the restaurant—small, and inviting looking, with a green awning over the tables outside.

When she told the owner of El Raitán about us, he congratulated Mark and Sam and led them to the head of a large table that accommodated all of us.

"We will make for you today, for this very special day in your lives, our most famous dish—*fabada*."

"Wait until you taste this," Rafaela said. "It's incredibly good."

"What's in it?" Mary Louise asked.

"It's a kind of stew made of sausages and beans."

"Nice light dish," I said. "I'm starving. Bring it on."

The owner treated us to six courses, each one delicious and much more than I could eat, but I tried each one: the fish soup, the *fabada*, some other kind of stew with kelp and vegetables, a potato filled with pork, and an onion stuffed with sausage, all served with white and red Spanish wines, and then desserts—a little cake, a crêpe, a cannoli.

Tina said, "We're supposed to dance tonight. I can't walk, much less dance."

"I think we'd better skip dinner," Pat said.

When we finally staggered out of the restaurant, we thanked the owner for the feast and for making it such a spectacular wedding reception.

Mary Louise managed to snag the recipe for *fabada*.

"May your days always be as blessed as this one," the owner said to Mark and Sam.

We still had time before we had to get on the bus again. I'm not really a shopper, but I saw a little boutique that sold pottery.

Janice, the champion shopper of our group, was already paying for something at the counter.

"What did you find, Jan?" I asked her.

"Look at this sangria pitcher, Gini. It's really beautiful. I'd never be able to find anything like this at home."

She held up a pitcher decorated with flowers in vivid shades of red, yellow, orange, and green.

"It's beautiful, Jan. Will you invite us all over for sangria when we get back home?"

"First I have to learn how to make it," she said.

"It's easy," I said. "Just pour a bottle of good red wine in there—Rioja is excellent—add around three ounces of orange juice, about two teaspoons of sugar—careful, you don't want it to be too sweet. Put in an ounce of triple sec. Add some ice. Stir it all up and drink it."

"You have to tell me again when we get home," she said. "I'll never remember."

"Count on it," I said.

I walked around the shop, trying to pick out a

pitcher. They were all so unusual, it was hard to choose. I finally decided on one that had blue flowers on a white background. Blue is my favorite color.

We left the shop and were just about to get on the bus when we heard bagpipes. We turned toward the sound and saw Mark blowing away on one.

"Mark, you play the bagpipes?" I said. "Is there no end to your talents?"

"I couldn't resist, Gini," he said. "This part of Spain has a very strong Celtic influence. They have their own bagpipes called *gaitas*. I'm of Scottish descent. I learned to play when I worked at a resort in Scotland one summer. I have one at home, but I loved this one when I saw it and decided to buy it."

"You going to put up with that, Sam?" I asked.

"I'll make him play it outdoors," Sam said. "Way, way, way outdoors."

We got back on the bus where Tina showed us the exquisite handmade lace tablecloth she had found in another shop.

"Your daughter Laurie will love that," I said.

Recipe for Fabada

1½ lb large white beans soaked overnight
1 lb salt pork
1lb ham hock
¼ tsp black peppercorns, ground
Pinch of saffron
½ tsp paprika
2 tbsps. olive oil
1 bay leaf
6 garlic cloves, minced
1 lb chorizos
1 onion

1. Put beans in a large pot of water and bring to a boil.

2. Add salt pork, ham hock, ground pepper, saffron, paprika, olive oil, bay leaf, and garlic. Simmer for an hour and a half.

3. Add chorizos and onion, peeled. Simmer for another hour to an hour and a half until the beans are soft.

4. Discard onion.

5. Slice the salt pork and the chorizos. Take the meat off the ham hock and cut it up into pieces for the stew.

6. Mix the beans and the chopped meat and serve.

Gini's photography tip: Get vertical once in a while instead of horizontal. (Good tip for your life too.)

Chapter 15

Guess Who?

When we were all seated on the bus and almost asleep after that fabulous lunch, Rafaela picked up her microphone. How she stayed so thin eating such incredible food all the time, I'll never know.

"Are you ready for Covadonga?" she asked.

"I think I'm ready for a nap," Janice said.

"Before you fall asleep," Rafaela said, "let me tell you the story of Covadonga because it's a fascinating one. Full of miracles and battles between the Muslims and the Catholic Spaniards in the seven hundreds. The Muslims pretty much took over Spain in the eighth century and considered it theirs, until a man from Covadonga named Don Pelayo led a revolt against them in the northern mountains of Asturias. He and his men were outnumbered by the Arabs, but they stationed themselves along the cliffs, hoping to be in a position to win back their territory. While they waited for the Muslims to attack, Don Pelayo went into the cave of Covadonga, which you will see today, where he had placed a statue of the Virgin Mary, and prayed to her for protection.

"According to legend, Mary answered his prayer swiftly and effectively. The Moors attacked, shooting arrows at Don Pelayo's forces. Incredibly, miraculously, Mary caused their arrows to turn back against them, killing the Muslims. The Spaniards attacked the fleeing Muslims and defeated them.

"As the Muslims were retreating, the blessed Virgin intervened again. The story goes that she called up a violent thunder storm with heavy rain that caused mudslides, sending boulders and trees tumbling down the mountain, crushing the retreating troops, who drowned in the Deva River below. The Catholic Spaniards had won decisively.

"Don Pelayo was crowned King of Asturias. King Alfonso had a monastery and chapel built on the site in honor of Our Lady of Covadonga. The bravery of this small band of Asturians led to other battles against the Arab invaders, and Spain eventually became a Christian land again."

Rafaela told the story so stirringly that we all gave a cheer at the end for the brave forces of Don Pelayo and the intervention of the Virgin Mary.

The bus stopped and Rafaela led us to the grotto where the men had defended Covadonga. There was a small chapel inside with a wooden statue of the Virgin in an ornate robe, a large circle of gold on her head, holding an elaborately dressed child. She was surrounded by lit candles. The inside of her robe was decorated with pictures of the three men who won this battle for Christianity. Nearby were the tombs of Don Pelayo and King Alfonso.

The others left to explore the rest of the town. I told Tina to go on ahead because I wanted to photograph this statue. It was difficult because the light was dim, but I thought my flash would be strong enough. I was circling the Virgin, looking at her from every angle, taking shots and experimenting to get just what I wanted. Absorbed in my photography, I didn't realize that the others had left the grotto.

I heard a small noise, like footsteps, in back of me. I assumed another tourist had entered.

"I'll be through in a minute," I said, not looking around. "I just want one more shot here."

"Oh, don't rush," an all-too-familiar woman's voice said. "Take your time."

Before I could react, I felt a scarf around my neck.

"You're not going to tell the inspector any more lies about me," Dora's gravelly voice said. "In fact, you're not going to tell him anything at all anymore."

She tightened the scarf, her knee in the middle of my back. I dropped my camera and struggled with her. I tried to get the scarf away from her, but she was too strong for me. With one last effort, I shoved my elbow into her stomach. She almost let go of the scarf but quickly regained her hold. In the instant when she loosened her grip, I said, "Dora, I can help you."

She stopped for a second. "What can you do?"

"There's a lawyer on the train. He's my friend. He'll help you."

She laughed. "Right. They'll have me declared insane and I'll spend the rest of my life in a mental hospital. No, thank you."

She tightened the scarf again. I stopped fighting. I went limp and fell to the ground. She let go of the brilliantly red scarf as I fell. I had just enough strength to roll back against her and knock her to the ground. We were almost on top of the statue of Mary. I grabbed one of the burning candles on the altar in front of her and smashed it into Dora's face. She screamed. I threw another candle at her, the flame catching her hair. She lost her grip on me. I managed to crawl to the entrance of the grotto and call for help.

Within seconds Mark and Sam were there. They grabbed Dora, covered her hair with a jacket to put out the flames, and pulled her out into the plaza.

They yelled to Rafaela to get the police.

I could not speak. I looked at this pathetic creature, crazed because of what life had done to her, and wondered how I was still alive.

I looked up at the statue of the Virgin in the grotto. "Thank you," I said silently. "You've done it again." I probably just imagined that she smiled.

After the police took Dora off to jail, I started to cry, retching, gut-wrenching, sobs from deep inside me. My friends surrounded me, but I couldn't stop. I was terrified. I had no faith at all that this woman would be shut up someplace for life. I knew she would get out of wherever they put her and come after me.

When I could speak again, I said, "I want to go home. I've had enough. No more. Please get me out of here. Out of this train, out of this country, out of this planet."

"Gini, what happened?" Tina asked.

"It was Dora," I said. "She followed me into the grotto and almost killed me."

"Are you all right, honey?" Mary Louise asked.

I looked at these dear friends and I couldn't stop crying.

"No, I'm not all right. I'll never be all right again. I'm going back to my house in New Jersey and I'm never leaving it. But there's no reason the rest of you can't finish the trip. You don't really need me. The four of you will be just fine."

"Do you really think we would go on without you?" Mary Louise said. "If you leave, we all leave." She looked around at the rest of my friends and they nodded vigorously.

"You're our heart and soul, Gini," Janice said. "Without you we lose the spark that makes us good. If you want to go home, we're coming with you."

"Are you going to be all right?" Pat said, tears in her eyes.

"I will be, sweetie. Don't worry about me."

"What else do I have to do?" she said.

Somehow I got on the bus and mercifully fell asleep.

I climbed back on the train, still shaken. Javier was there in our cabin waiting for me.

"Gini, I'm so sorry," he said. "I didn't get your message until this morning. I drove to Covadonga, but I was too late. What was it you were going to tell me?"

"I finally figured it out," I said. "The way Dora acted when I returned her ring kept nagging at me. I couldn't understand why she was so frantic about getting it back. Then I remembered there was a kind of dust inside when I opened it. I remembered that she had the ring on when she asked Shambless for his autograph. I was sure she must have put the oleander powder in his wine when he looked down to sign her menu. Later, she was afraid Steve had filmed her when he took pictures in the restaurant, so she stole his camera and then killed him too."

"How did she know you knew all this?" the inspector asked.

"She didn't really know, but she was afraid I would find out after the tea party fiasco and my bringing you to question her. She wasn't going to take any chances, so she waited for me in the cave and almost succeeded in getting rid of me for good." I shuddered.

"How did she think she would get away after she killed you?" the inspector asked.

"I suppose she thought she'd just pick up her scarf and stroll out of the cave and join the other passengers. When they found my body, she'd act as horrified as everyone else and play the tourist until she had to kill the next person. She's totally insane, Inspector."

"I feel responsible," he said. "The reason I didn't take any calls last night was because I had an emergency at my home. One of my children was in the hospital and I was there with my wife."

"Your wife?" I said. How many more surprises did this day have in store? "You're married?" I asked. "Does Janice know that?"

"No," the inspector said. "I will tell her today." He saw the expression on my face. "Janice didn't think we were going to get married."

"Even so," I said. "How could you not tell her?"

"That's between Janice and me, Gini," he said. "Let me tell her, please. Now let's get back to you. Are you all right?"

"I will be," I said. "But tell me about your child. Is he or she all right?"

"He will be," Javier said. "My son suffered a concussion playing in a game at school, but they got him to the hospital right away. He'll be home tomorrow. But what about you?"

"I'll be fine as soon as I get back home, as far away from Dora as I can get. I'm not at all sure she won't turn up tomorrow or the next day."

"She'll never be able to get to you again," he said. "But you'll have to help."

"If you mean I have to see her again, forget it."

"I'm afraid you'll have to testify at her trial. If you don't, we have no way to prove anything."

"But the bag of oleander leaves . . . her fingerprints . . . DNA . . . there have to be other things that will convict her."

"Without your testimony, a good lawyer could get her off, or at least get her a brief sentence and then . . ."

"And then, she'll try again? Is that what you're telling me?"

"Yes. Don't forget, Gini, we're talking about

two murders and one attempted murder here, not just about Shambless."

"I knew she killed Steve, but I couldn't figure out how," I said.

"She must have sneaked into his room and put oleander powder in the pitcher of water next to his bed. He wasn't very good about locking his door. The poison worked right away."

"Javier, I'm getting out of here as soon as I can," I said. "I've had enough."

"I need you to file a deposition and testify at the trial. That could be months from now. You can finish this trip. A week in San Sebastian would be lifesaving for you. Then you can return to America until the trial."

"I can't, Javier," I said. "I'm terrified that she will somehow escape and come after me again."

"That's why it's crucial that you testify against her and make sure she is put away for life and can never come after you."

"Do I have to decide this minute?"

"No, of course not. Think about it. We'll talk later."

"As if I could think about anything else," I said.

"I need to find Janice," the inspector said. "As I mentioned before, I need to tell her about my wife. Do you know where she is?"

"I think she said she was going to the bar," I said. "Try there."

After Javier left, Tina sat down beside me on

the bed and put her arm around me. I needed that hug.

"I don't know what's wrong with me, Tina," I said, holding on to her hand. "I never used to be afraid of anything and now—look at me—I'm afraid of my own shadow. I'm really scared of a little gray-haired woman who wants to kill me."

"Who wouldn't be?" Tina asked. "You've been through a lot. Give yourself a break. You'll be all right. I know you. But right now don't beat yourself up."

"I don't remember you turning into a frightened ninny during our Moscow cruise," I said.

"Are you kidding?" Tina said. "I woke up screaming, with horrible nightmares for months after that. Peter was always there, holding me, calming me, telling me I was safe, until finally I could sleep through the night. It does go away, but it takes a while."

"I think it will take the rest of my life," I said.

Gini's photography tip: Say cheese everybody! (Especially Cabrales blue cheese from Asturias.)

Chapter 16

And Then What Happened?

After dinner on our last night, Tina gathered us around a table in the lounge, full of comfortable chairs and passengers sipping drinks or coffee, and said, "Okay, guys, it's travel tip time. I need to write a list of pointers for anyone who might be taking this train trip across Green Spain. Got any suggestions?"

"If somebody loses a ring," I said, "let it stay lost."

Laughter from my loyal fans.

"We'll all remember that one, Gini," Tina said. "Now I need some from non-almost-murder victims."

"May and September are the best months to take this trip," Denise said. "The summers can be really hot and part of the winter months freezing cold. I thought it was comfortable walking around this first week in September."

"I agree," Tina said. "Eduardo, come join us, please. We're trying to give the readers of my magazine some good advice if they plan to take this train. What do you think?"

"Make sure the Happy Hoofers are going to be the entertainers when you go," Eduardo said, smiling. "Especially if there is a murder that needs solving." He looked at each of us, smiling. "One thing that is very important to tell your readers is that we have Internet access and phone service to the United States. Also, they don't need a visa to come to Spain."

"What about clothes? What would you tell them to pack?" Pat asked.

"You can live in jeans and sweaters on the train," Eduardo said. "You might want to get a little more dressed up when we go to a restaurant. A skirt or really nice pants for the ladies, perhaps a jacket for the gentlemen."

"That will be a relief for the honeymooners who read my magazine," Tina said. "Young people like to be casual."

"Don't forget to tell them about wheelchairs, Eduardo," a woman in the back called out. She was the mother of the boy with muscular dystrophy.

"Thank you, señora," Eduardo said. "We are very proud of the fact that our train is now equipped with ramps for people using wheelchairs and the bathrooms are wider."

"We could never have made this trip if you hadn't done that," she said. "It's still hard getting in and out of restaurants here and pushing a chair over the cobblestone streets. There are very few curb cuts."

"I am sorry for that," Eduardo said. "We were slow to make those improvements here in Spain. I hope they will expand the program to make it easier for you and your son."

"Well, this gives me a good start," Tina said. "But I could still use some more if anything occurs to any of you."

We ordered some tea and cakes. While we were waiting, Cynthia, the lady whose son, Paul, was in a wheelchair, approached me shyly.

"I hope you didn't mind my interrupting you," she said.

"I'm so glad you did," I said. "You made a very good point. An essential one, in fact."

"I really wanted to talk to you about that woman, that Dora. I couldn't believe she was a murderer. When she spoke to me, she seemed like such a nice harmless person. Not crazy enough to poison people."

"You didn't look at her eyes, Mom," Paul said. "Sometimes she had this really wild look in them when she was talking about her little girl. She scared me."

"How come you never said anything about that, Paul?" his mother asked.

"I just thought I was imagining it," Paul said. "You know, her little girl died. That must have been terrible for her."

His mother was silent. He didn't see the tears in her eyes, but I did.

"How are you enjoying the trip, Paul?" I asked. "Is it interesting for someone your age?"

"It's great," he said. "Especially the food. The only thing is . . ."

"What?" I asked.

"Oh, it happens all the time. I should be used to it by this time."

"Tell me."

"It's just that people don't talk to you when you're in a wheelchair. It's as if they don't think we have a mind or opinions. I shouldn't complain. It's just a fact of life. But I wish people knew that a disability is really a small part of who a person is."

"I can certainly see that in talking to you," I said. "I think you have to start the conversations yourself. Just plow right in. You'll be surprised at how quickly people respond."

"Maybe I'll try it with that girl over there," he said, aiming his wheelchair at Michele, who was flipping through her phone with a bored expression.

I watched as he talked to her. Her face lit up and she put her phone back in her tote bag. They were soon absorbed in each other—probably talking about computers.

"That's a great guy you have there," I said to his mother.

"I'm glad he was loaned to me for a while," she said.

"Me too," I said.

I saw Janice standing by the bar and joined her.

"Hi, Jan," I said. "Where's Javier?"

"Probably home with his wife," she said. She didn't look at me.

Ah, he told her.

"What do you mean, his wife?" I said, feigning ignorance.

"You heard me, Gini." She put another spoonful of sugar in her coffee. "

"Did you know all along that he was married? You've always said you'll never go out with married men." And she's supposed to be the one who is an actress! I'm not so bad myself.

Janice put a hand on my arm. "Take it easy, Gini. I didn't know he was married. He never mentioned it until last night after we got back on the train. Right after he talked to you. He told me he cares for me a lot, but that he could never marry me because he already had a wife."

"What did you say?" I asked. I knew I was making her uncomfortable, but, as usual, I couldn't stop. There's something about me that always needs an answer.

"Nothing, at first. I was stunned. I did ask him why he never mentioned her before. He said they weren't in love anymore, but he's a Catholic. Even if he got a divorce, he could never marry again. We could live together, but we couldn't marry. Somehow, that just didn't appeal to me." I couldn't read the expression on her face. Sometimes it's hard with Jan. I didn't really know if she was heartbroken or didn't care. I settled on somewhere in between.

"Oh, Jan, I'm sorry," I said, to be safe. "How do you feel?"

"Relieved, more than anything, Gini," she said. She smiled at me. "There were lots of other reasons it probably wouldn't have worked out, so this gives me a good excuse. I think he's relieved too."

"Didn't I see you with Tom before?" I asked. One more thing I had to know the answer to. I pushed my cup forward on the bar for another refill. I should have ordered decaf. Probably wouldn't get to sleep for hours.

"Yes, he wants to see me when we're back to New York. He said he's breaking up with Sylvia."

I almost choked on my coffee. "You're kidding," I said. Much as I disliked Sylvia—once thought she might be the murderer, for heaven's sake—I just thought obedient Tom would stay with her because it was easier that way. "Are you going to see him?" I asked. "I can't keep up with you."

Janice shrugged. "Listen, Gini," she said. "I can't keep up with myself. I know, it sounds crazy, but he said he just couldn't live with her anymore. That she was too negative. He said he really loves me and has loved me since we were in that play in New York."

"So . . ."

"I don't know, Gini. I'll certainly see him when we get back home. But who knows whether he is really going to divorce Sylvia or if it's just a temporary split. I want to give it a chance. Do you think I'm crazy?"

"Of course not, Jan. I think you're right to go slowly."

"Look," Janice said. "There's Mike and Mary Louise over there in the corner on the couch. What's going on with them?"

"Hard to tell," I said. "Let's go find out.

"You go ahead, Gini," Janice said. "I feel funny asking them if they're, what, having an affair. I'll see you later."

Mike and Mary Louise were close together in another part of the car talking to each other. I went over to them. I had to ask them if they still planned to get married when we got back home. I was afraid of the answer.

They stopped talking when I approached.

Mary Louise saw the worried expression on my face, and answered my question before I could ask it.

"It's okay, Gini," she said. "Mike and I have talked it over, and we realize this has all happened too fast. I'll stay with George—at least for now—and we'll see what happens."

The look of relief on my face was so blatant, they both laughed. "I didn't know you felt so strongly about this, Gini," Mike said. "Do you think it would be a terrible thing for us to get married?"

"Oh, Mike," I said. "You're a really good guy. It's just that I know how much George loves Mary Louise—even if he isn't very good at showing it sometimes."

"Sometimes!" Mary Louise said. "Lately it's more like never."

"I know," I said, "but I think you're right to give him another chance."

Mike put his arm around Mary Louise. His face was sad. "I really love her, Gini."

My heart went out to this decent, truly good person.

Just then, Denise came over to us.

"Gini, could I talk to you for a minute alone," she said.

"Of course," I said, following her to a chair across the room.

"I have to tell you something, Gini," she said. "It's been bothering me."

"It's about the church, isn't it, Denise?" I asked.

"Yes," she said. "I don't know why I lied to you about being there that morning. I guess because we weren't supposed to leave the train. I had this strong yearning to be in a church, to talk to God in His house. I was so confused about a lot of things. Worried about my son. And I felt so grateful to have met Pat. I didn't know what to do about her either. Should I see her after we got back? I always talk to Him when I'm troubled, but that day I needed a church. That was such a beautiful one. The music was healing. You understand? I just didn't want to share it with anyone. That's why I didn't tell you. I'm sorry."

"No need to apologize, Denise," I said. "I understand perfectly. I didn't want to leave that church either, it was so full of His spirit. Are you going to continue seeing Pat when we get back home?"

"I'm not sure. She's a wonderful person. But I have to focus on getting my son adjusted to a new school and a new group of friends. We'll talk about it."

Michele was sitting nearby talking to Paul.

"Gini," she said. "I meant to tell you. I'm meeting Jonathan in Boston after I get back to talk to him about testing some of our talking wearables. He's a great guy and I look forward to seeing him again. Thanks for introducing us."

"I'm so glad, Michele. I guess we didn't persuade you to give up your career in technology to become a dancer. Too bad. You're good."

"You came close, Gini, you and your hoofer pals. I envy you because you always look like you're having such a great time when you're dancing."

"It's true, Michele. It's liberating. Like pure joy. Time out from our regular lives that have to be more serious."

"How about one last fling," Michele said.

She grabbed me and we started to sing "New York, New York." In a flash, Mary Louise, Tina, Pat, and Janice ran over to join us. We locked arms and kicked left to right, singing our hearts out and making that room ring with the love of life.

A blast of applause from our fellow passengers sent us off to bed and dreams of being back home again.

Chapter 17

All Tapped Out

We left for home the next day. I returned to Spain in a few months to testify at Dora's trial. She was found insane and sentenced to life in a mental hospital.

I've never quite recovered from my experience in Green Spain. Somehow I lost my taste for tea. Alex and I made plans to leave for India to try to adopt my little girl.

Pat moved in with Denise. They've been happy together. Their relationship didn't affect Pat's practice, which included other men and women who were dealing with the fact that they're gay. They were finding out that being a couple had a whole new set of problems that never came up when they just lived together. Pat has never been happier. Denise gave up drinking—she never drank very much anyway—and Pat has stayed sober. Denise's son has accepted Pat as a positive part of his new life.

Tom separated from Sylvia after the trip on the train. He and Janice have cautiously renewed their friendship. It looks like it's becoming more than a friendship, but for the moment they're just enjoying each other. Tom left the soap. It was too difficult working with Sylvia, who was the producer. He was happily acting off-Broadway in a challenging new play. Janice was writing a book about the Gypsy Robes with her daughter.

Mary Louise changed her mind about divorcing George and marrying Mike. She sees Mike from time to time, as a friend.

Tina was still trying to decide whether to marry Peter or not, but when she got an offer for us to dance on the Bateau Mouche, she couldn't resist. *Vive la France!*

I changed my mind about giving up dancing forever.

Want to come along?

Don't miss the next delightful mystery
featuring the Happy Hoofers

CANCANS, CROISSANTS, AND CASKETS

Coming from Kensington in Fall 2015

High-kicking actress Janice Rogers takes over
as narrator as the five fabulous fiftysomething
friends dance their way to Paris, the magical
city of lights—and into a murder plot that's
as multilayered as a French pastry!

Keep reading to enjoy a sample excerpt . . .

Chapter 1

Bonjour, Paris

Why we decided to arrive in Paris on the fourteenth of July, one of France's biggest holidays, I'll never know. We call it Bastille Day because it's the anniversary of the day in 1789 when the French stormed the prison, the Bastille, to liberate the political prisoners and to celebrate the unity of France, but the French call it *La Fête Nationale* or *le quatorze juillet*, which just means The National Holiday or the fourteenth of July. It's a day of parades and closed shops and picnics, and fireworks at night. A day when all of France has a huge party. Kind of like our Fourth of July. A lot like our fourth of July.

I'm Janice Rogers, and I'm going to tell you the story of our Paris adventure that took me and my four best friends down the beautiful Seine River and into the heart of a murder mystery that we ended up solving—but not without some danger.

We were hired to dance on a dinner cruise on a Bateau Mouche for seven nights. It would have made sense to come at least one day before the fourteenth, but Tina Powell, our leader, couldn't get a flight for the five of us Happy Hoofers until the evening before and since Paris is six hours ahead of us, we arrived early the morning of the fourteenth.

Before we left, Gini complained that we wouldn't have time to rehearse, but Tina assured her. "We know what we're going to do," she said. "We've rehearsed it enough. All we have to do is show up and dance. Everybody will be too full of wine to notice if we make any mistakes anyway. And we'll be part of one of France's biggest celebrations."

We believed her. What did we know? Who thought before the night was over and the last firework burst into the Paris sky that someone would be dead? Who thinks of murder on the biggest, most joyful holiday in all of France on Bastille Day? Excuse me, *La Fête Nationale.*

This was my first time back in Paris since my honeymoon with my second husband. It was still the same magical city it was twenty-five years before. No matter what they do to Paris, it never loses the beauty and charm that makes it different from all other cities in the world.

"There it is," Gini said, her voice almost a whisper. "The good old Eiffel Tower. We're in Paris. My Paris. I can't believe we're here."

The five of us Happy Hoofers were loaded into a van on our way from Orly Airport to the apartment we had rented for a week on Boulevard Montparnasse, on the left bank, while we danced every night on the Bateau Mouche. I was glad we were going to be in an apartment instead of a hotel, because I thought it would be more relaxing.

For Gini Miller, it was a real homecoming. She studied photography for a year in Paris after she graduated from college. Whenever anyone mentioned France or French anything, her face radiated a glow that told us exactly how she felt about this city. "It was a year when I could improvise my life, Jan," she once told me. "I time-stepped my way through that city of lights, drank sweet vermouth with a twist at the Select café with artists and writers and actors and directors and . . ." She paused for breath. "I was in love with someone different every week." She became an award-winning filmmaker because of what she learned in this incredible city.

"Does all this bring back memories, Gini?" I asked as our cab turned onto a broad avenue lined with canopied sidewalk cafes.

"Wonderful memories, Jan," she said.

I love Paris, too, but my view of it is slightly

marred by the memory of my second husband, Derek, who wasn't all that great after the honeymoon. He spoiled Paris for me because I couldn't help thinking about the way he turned out when we got back home. That marriage only lasted two years, definitely two years too long.

"Look," Mary Louise Temple said, pointing to the glass pyramid we were passing. "The Louvre."

"We have to go there," Pat Keeler said. "There's a fantastic exhibit of Renaissance sculpture. Denise said we absolutely must not miss that."

"We're going to see everything," Tina, our planner extraordinaire, said. "I've got a list."

"Are we dancing every night?" I asked.

"That's the plan," Tina said.

"Look," Gini said, her face reflecting her delight. "There it is—the Arc de Triomphe. That's Paris personified. We're on the Champs-Élysées. Tina, I love you forever for getting this gig for us. How did you do it anyway?"

"It was the publicity about our gig on that train in Spain that landed us in all the papers because the talk show host who was murdered was so famous. We got offers from everywhere. I'm glad we decided to stick with gigs closer to home during the winter. But when this offer came in, it seemed like the best one for a midsummer getaway."

"Where else could we have gone?" I asked.

"Camden, New Jersey, or Winnipeg," Tina said, trying not to smile.

"Tough choice," Pat said.

The taxi moved along the busy wide avenue. People were lined up four and five deep on either side.

"What's going on?" Gini asked the taxi driver in French.

"*Madame, c'est le quatorze juillet,*" he said and explained what was happening in French to her.

Gini translated his words for us. "It's Bastille day," she said. "They're going to close down the Champs in an hour because of the parade. People have been waiting there since early this morning."

We passed The Gap, Disney, Hugo Boss, Sephora, and Cartier along the crowded sidewalks. There was even a McDonald's. I'll never get used to a McDonald's on Paris's most glamorous, elegant avenue.

We crossed the Pont Neuf onto the Left Bank. The artistic, bohemian part of Paris. The cafes were crowded. The red, white and blue French flag flew from every building. We drove down a narrow street past the Sorbonne, past the Jardin du Luxembourg, to Boulevard Montparnasse. Everywhere we saw flowers in ceramic planters, graceful shade trees, and people walking dogs that looked clean and well-trained.

"There's La Coupole," I said, pointing to the red awning that was almost a block long. "Hemingway's restaurant. Can we eat there?"

"Of course," Tina said. "It's only a block from our apartment. See. That's where we're going to stay. The one with the balconies overlooking the boulevard."

"I lived right next door when I was here," Gini said. "That's my café across the street. The Select. I practically lived there. It's just the same."

She was almost dancing in her seat in the van. The rest of us had been to Paris once or twice, but it didn't have the same meaning for us as it did for Gini. I envied her having lived there.

Tina paid the cab driver a bunch of euros, and we dragged all our bags and assorted belongings to the door of our new temporary home. Tina punched in the entry code and held the door for us as we filed into the foyer. Another code opened the inside door and we squeezed into the glass elevator to the third floor.

There was one other apartment on this floor. Tina stuck the key in the lock and after some maneuvering and pulling and pushing, opened the door.

We had only seen pictures online of this place, but it was perfect. It had a large living room with a couch that converted into a bed, several big black, comfortable-looking leather chairs, a coffee table, a basket full of books in English—nice touch—a T.V. and a dining table. Off the living room, there was a roomy, bright kitchenette with a combination washer-dryer, a dishwasher, fridge, stove, two sinks and cabinets with glass doors full of plates, glasses and serving dishes.

There were two bedrooms, a room with a toilet, and a room with a shower and sink and heated towel racks complete with thick, terry towels. In France, the toilet and the shower are usually in separate rooms.

I could have used another shower stall, but this was Paris. I was grateful for one. We'd just have to bathe in shifts. One bathroom was the only thing particularly French about this apartment, except for the view from the little balcony on one side of the living room. That was spectacular. We could look down on Boulevard Montparnasse and watch people sipping coffee at the Select across the street, men and women hurrying by on their way to work, cars going by. Very Paris.

The view from our bedrooms was of other apartments close by. So close, in fact, we kept the blinds down when we were dressing or running around in our underwear. The blinds opened and closed with a remote control, which took some getting used to, but they were fun.

"What do you think, gang?" Tina asked. "Are we okay with this?"

"Who gets to sleep in the living room?" Pat, our practical, always thinking family therapist asked.

"Any volunteers?" Tina asked.

"I'll sleep in here," Mary Louise said. "I don't mind." She's our peace-at-any-price Hoofer. We all love her and take advantage of her good nature all the time. She doesn't seem to mind, so we keep doing it. People treat you the way you let yourself be treated, I've discovered in this life as an actress, director, wife, and mother.

You wouldn't think it to look at me, but I'm tough. I had my daughter when I was seventeen, divorced her father a year later, and supported my child as a waitress while I auditioned for acting jobs in New York. I'm blond with a little help from my hairdresser. People tell me I'm beautiful, but I don't really believe them because my mother never missed a chance to tell me that I was "average looking" when I was growing up. She thought telling me I was pretty would spoil me.

My father was too busy chasing after other women to pay much attention to me. Before he left my mother for a younger woman when I was twelve, he would occasionally take me to movies and baseball games at Yankee Stadium. I adored him. I guess I've been looking for him ever since, through three marriages and countless love affairs.

My daughter and I have had some rocky times, probably because we're too much alike. She didn't talk to me for a long time, until last year when she asked me to collaborate on a book with her about the Gypsy Robes on Broadway, a tradition among chorus dancers in musicals. I cherish my time with her.

Gini and I unpacked in the bedroom we would share. I plopped down on one of the beds to test it. It had the kind of firm mattress I like. There was no dresser, just a stack of baskets to keep our things in. No closet either. We would have to hang our clothes in the closet by the entrance door to the apartment. The mirror was weird—sort of wavy and distorted—but I checked and there was a good one in the bathroom and a full-length mirror in the living room. Not great, but you can't have everything.

I was grateful that I would be sharing a room with Gini. I like her. She always says what she means. That can be like a kick in the stomach at times, but I prefer her directness to Mary Louise's attempt to find sunshine in every disaster that comes our way. I love Mary Louise dearly, just like I love our whole gang, but I need a rest from her sometimes.

Tina and Pat shared the other bedroom. It was almost as bare bones as ours, but there was a dresser and a mirror that you could actually see yourself in. Tina gets along with everybody. That's why she's our leader. She's travel editor at a bridal magazine and is the most organized of all of us. She's the best one to deal with Pat's never-ending search for flaws in every situation. Pat's philosophy is that if you find things that need to be fixed ahead of time and fix them, you'll never have any problems. I don't think life works like that. Half the time disasters that you think are going to happen don't happen, and even if they do, they're never what you expected. They just land on you with a thump and you figure out what to do then. You improvise. Maybe because I'm an actress, I'm pretty good at improvising.

It was ten in the morning in Paris, but my body clock was still back in New Jersey set at four A.M. I was jet lagged. I conked out on the twin bed in the room I shared with Gini. The last thing I saw before I drifted into sleep was the framed historic map of Paris hanging on the opposite wall. *Oh, you beautiful city,* I thought. *For one week you are mine.*

We woke up ravenously hungry and headed across the street to The Select café for omelets and coffee or tea or hot chocolate for me. Paris bustled by us on this glorious morning in July. There's something about sitting at an outdoor table at a café in Paris that is totally different from doing the same thing in New York. It's more relaxed somehow. The other people at tables near us were sipping coffee in a leisurely way, talking to each other, reading the newspaper. None of them looked as if they were eating as fast as they could so they could get back to work before anyone noticed they were gone the way they do back home. It was my kind of place.

"What time do we dance tonight, Tina?" I asked.

"At 8:30, but we have to check in at our bateau this morning and find out who's in charge, what kind of music system they have, what else we have to do," she said.

Well-fed and fairly presentable looking, we headed for the nearest metro. "Let's get a carnet," Gini said.

My French is limited to "*oui*," "*non*," "*bonjour*", "*combien?*" and "*ou est la toilette?*" so I asked Gini what a carnet was.

"A booklet of metro tickets instead of one ticket at a time," she said. "It's much cheaper."

We checked the map for the nearest stop to our boat, bought a carnet, and jumped on the next metro. It was a lot cleaner than the subways in New York, but then, what isn't? It was also a lot easier to find your stop because of the easy-to-follow maps everywhere in the system. I love New York, but their subway system could use a lot of help.

Our Bateau Mouche was anchored a short distance from our metro stop. It was a long, sleek boat with glass windows all around the lower portion and an open deck at the top. Several other Bateaux Mouches were anchored in front of it. The river teemed with other sight-seeing boats sailing by during the holiday week in Paris.

"*Bonjour,*" the woman behind the ticket desk said. "*Je regrette, mais il n'y a pas un bateau cette apres-midi.*"

Even those of us who don't speak much French understood that she was telling us there was no tour that afternoon.

Gini explained to her in French that we were looking for Henri Fouchet, the person in charge of the bateau. That we were the Happy Hoofers, the entertainment on the dinner cruises for the coming week.

The woman pointed to the ramp leading to the boat and told us to ask for Monsieur Fouchet when we boarded.

We could hear the music as we walked onto the boat. Waiters were setting up the tables lining both sides of the boat, each one next to a floor-to-ceiling glass window so the passengers could see the monuments in Paris during the evening cruise that night. Each table had red, white, and blue flowers. Stuck in the middle of the bouquet was a little French flag with its wide blue vertical stripe on the left, a white band in the middle, and the red one on the right. There was a stairway leading from this enclosed part of the ship to the open deck on top.

"*Bonjour,*" one of waiters said to us as we twirled a couple of times in time to the music playing at the prow of the bateau. You couldn't help it. I couldn't anyway. It was an Edith Piaf song, "Padam, Padam," the beat so strong you had to move your body along with it. I was really getting into it, when Tina put her arm around my waist and led me toward the prow. "Save it for later, Jan," she said.

Four men were sitting on simple wooden chairs. One played a trumpet, one a cello, one was on keyboard, and the other on drums. They segued into a lively version of "New York, New York" and played even louder when they saw us. We linked arms and swung into a tap routine that showed off our bodies to their best advantage. Dancing is one of the best ways to stay in shape and we were definitely toned. We were wearing halter tops and jeans and sandals in the summertime heat. It was our kind of music.

The men played faster and faster and we kept up with them. Finally with a triumphant blast of sound they ended the song and applauded us as we bowed to them.

"Bonjour," the man on trumpet said to us. "*Vous êtes les Happy Hoofers de New York, n'est-ce pas?*" He was in his forties, his hair rumpled, a stubble of beard on his chin making him sexy.

"*Oui,*" Gini said. "Do you speak English? I speak French, but my friends only speak English."

"Of course," he said. "We have to know English because a lot of our passengers are from America. Welcome. I'm Jean."

The other musicians introduced themselves. The drummer was young, in his twenties, his eyes bleary. His name was Yves. "Hey," he said.

Claude, the cellist, was the cleanest, with neatly combed, long brown hair, clean-shaven, and dark brown eyes that looked us all over and came back to me. He saluted me and said, "Later."

While the cellist and I were looking each other over, the keyboard guy grinned and said, "Where you from?" He was a little overweight but cute anyway. He had a mischievous smile and twinkly eyes, longish hair. Something about him made me think he wasn't French.

"New Jersey," Gini said. "You're not from here, are you?"

"How'd you guess?" he said. "I was born in Brooklyn. I'm Ken."

"How long have you been here?" she asked.

"A couple of years," he said. "I'll go home one of these days. But not yet."

Looking at him, I knew he'd never go back. Once Paris gets a hold on you, you never want to leave.

"Is Monsieur Fouchet around?" Tina asked.

"He should be back any minute," Jean said. "You want to give us an idea of what kind of music you need? They just told us you tap dance."

"We thought we'd dance to the music made

famous by a different French entertainer each of the five nights we'll be here. Edith Piaf, Yves Montand, Charles Trenet, Maurice Chevalier, and Charles Aznavour."

"You're really going back there, aren't you?" Jean said.

"Too far back for you?" Tina asked.

"No, most of the people who can afford this dinner cruise are old and rich," Jean said. "They come here for the music they remember from the two weeks they came to Paris when they were young. We can play that music with our eyes closed."

"Allo," a husky woman's voice called to us. "You must be the Happy Hoofers," she said with an adorable French accent.

We turned around to see a slim, brown-skinned woman with short, dark hair and large brown eyes that dominated her face. She reminded me a little of Rihanna. She was wearing a sleeveless, flowery dress, carrying a blond shih-tzu with black ears. It was impossible to guess her age. She could have been anywhere from twenty-five to forty-five. She looked so French, I expected the band to strike up "The Marseillaise."

"Bonjour," Tina said. "We are the Happy Hoofers. You must be Suzette Millet. You're going to sing while we dance, right?"

"Oui," she said. "I will do the French songs from the fifties. First night, Edith Piaf? Ça va?"

"*Trés bien*," Tina said. "Will you do 'Les Feuilles Mortes'? That's my absolute favorite."

"How could I not do 'Autumn Leaves'?" Suzette said. She put her little dog on a chair nearby and started to sing the song that I had heard many times about two lovers who separate and their love fades away like footprints in the sand. It always makes me sad to hear that song. It did so now listening to that voice that was an echo of Piaf's. Strong, rolling her r's, passionate.

When she finished, she said, "But that's too slow for you to dance to. 'Milord' would be perfect." She sang it, first full-voiced and Edith Piafian on the chorus, then slower and sadder for the verse. We linked arms and time stepped and mini-grapevined to this story-song of a lost gentleman, comforted by a French woman of very little virtue but much compassion, as she invites him into her room away from the cold and loneliness. Shuffling and step-stepping we told the story with our feet and our arms and our love of this song, so French, so Piaf.

"Great song, Suzette," Tina said," But let's do that one second. I'd rather start out with 'Les Grands Boulevards,' if that's okay with you. I love Yves Montand—that was his song. Let's work out a program and we'll practice on this stage, which is small, but big enough, I think."

" 'Les Grands Boulevards' is absolutely *parfait*," Suzette said. "One of my favorites." She looked up and her whole face changed, became livelier when she saw the man who had just boarded the bateau.

"Oh, Henri. Allo, *mon cher*," she said. She greeted a man with dark hair and sexy eyes who kissed Suzette on both cheeks. "*Ça va, cherie?*" he said. He was casually dressed in a white shirt open at the neck and black pants. Except for a slight paunch, he was in excellent shape.

"Ah, the Americans have arrived, I see," he said when he could tear himself away from Suzette. "*Bonjour.*"

"Monsieur Fouchet?" Tina said. "I'm Tina Powell, and these are the Happy Hoofers who are going to dance on your bateau this week." She pointed first to Gini, who shook his hand and rattled off a long paragraph in French that seemed to please him.

"Your French is excellent, Madame," he said. "Where did you learn it?"

"I studied here when I was young," she said.

His attention shifted to me. His eyes widened. "And who is this?" he asked. I detected a little too much interest in his eager expression.

"Janice Rogers," I said, moving back a few steps before he could welcome me to the boat with a kiss.

"*Enchanté*," he said, kissing my hand.

Tina had to prod him gently to introduce him to Pat and Mary Louise, who were trying not to laugh. They've seen this happen a hundred times, and for some reason, they don't resent me for it. Pat once said to me, "Your looks are a fact of life, and we get more jobs because of it. Anyway, we love you."

"We are very pleased to have you with us this week," Henri said, addressing all of us. "As you know, your first performance will be tonight, le quatorze Juillet. One of our biggest holidays. We have fireworks, celebrations, songs, dancing, and we fill every seat on the Bateau Mouche on this night. You will be the perfect entertainment." His eyes fastened on me again. I thought I saw Suzette frown. She looked away quickly and hugged her little dog closer to her.

"*Tiens, tiens, tiens,*" a low, rather growly voice, said. We turned to see a woman with a face that could only be French. Her complexion was flawless, her make-up subtle but perfectly applied to show off her blue-green eyes. She had a longish nose, high cheekbones, thin lips, and an expression that said, "I am here now. Don't mess with me."

"Ah, *chérie,*" Monsieur Fouchet said. "Come meet our Happy Hoofers who arrived today. Hoofers, this is my wife Madeleine."

She did not smile, just looked at each of us as if deciding whether she approved of us or not.

Tina took over in her graceful, charming way, holding out her hand to Madame Fouchet. "We are so happy to be here, madame," she said. "We love being in Paris, and we are grateful to have the chance to perform on this Bateau Mouche."

Madame Fouchet took Tina's hand and her expression softened slightly. "I look forward to seeing you dance," she said.

Tina introduced her to the rest of us. She paused before she shook my hand, her eyes appraising me coldly. "You are quite beautiful," she said, surprising me.

"Thank you, madame," I managed to say. "That's very kind of you."

She walked over to Suzette, kissed her on both cheeks and patted the shih-tzu. "*Bonjour, chouchou*," she said, moving on to greet her husband.

"*Alors*, Henri," she said. "You are coming with me to arrange the flags on deck?" It was not a question.

"*Mais oui*," he said. "Mesdames," he said to us, "You will be here by seven tonight? The guests board at 7:45, and our bateau sails at 8:30. We tour until eleven and then anchor near the Eiffel Tower to watch the fireworks on the top deck. *Entendu?*"

"We will be here," Tina said.

Madame Fouchet glanced briefly at the musicians, I thought she looked a little longer at Jean the trumpet player, but I was probably wrong.

She took her husband's arm and headed for the stairway to the upper deck.

"One more time," Ken, the ex-pat keyboard guy said, smiling at me and swinging into "Aupres de ma Blonde." Even I knew that meant "Next to My Blonde." Things were looking up.

Janice's fashion tip: Unless you're 16 with gorgeous legs, don't wear shorts in Paris.

Chapter 2

Fireworks

We worked out a routine with Suzette and the band and left the boat to explore Paris before we had to return to the apartment and dress for our performance that night.

Mary Louise and Tina headed for the Champs-Élysées and shopping. "July is the best month of the year for sales," Tina said. Gini wanted to take photos of the children riding the carousel in the Tuileries. Pat said she would find the nearest Jardin de café and watch the people go by. "Don't worry, guys," she said. "I'm only drinking lemonade."

Pat hadn't had anything alcoholic to drink for more than a year. We worried a little that Paris and all its wine would lure her back to drinking again, so we were relieved to hear the word "lemonade."

I wanted to go back to Montmartre to relive some of the memories of my honeymoon there with Derek. I hopped on a Metro, got off at Abbesses and walked up the steep, winding street that led to the Place du Tertres just below the Sacré Coeur.

As I climbed up that hill, I remembered the day Derek and I made the same trek when we were in Paris on our honeymoon. It was a beautiful, warm day in June. We were holding hands and stopping to kiss every few yards. We were so in love. I met him when we worked together in a play off Broadway. He seemed to be fine with my having a little girl. It wasn't until we got back home that he made it clear that he didn't want her around.

But on that day in Montmartre we were halfway up the hill, when some music drifted out of an open window. I think it was "April in Paris." Derek took me in his arms and we danced right there in the middle of that little street. We felt like we were the stars of a romantic movie. I thought we would be in love like this forever. I've learned that "forever" doesn't exist in my life, no matter how much I think it's going to.

On this day, twenty-five years later, I was all alone. No one to dance with. No one to tell me I was the most wonderful woman in the world. No one to kiss me and dance with me in the middle of the street. I sat down at an outdoor table in one of the cafes and breathed in the feel of Paris. I missed being in love.

"What would you like, madame?" the waiter said. He was a thin, dapper man with a carefully trimmed mustache.

"A glass of white wine, please," I said. "A sauvignon blanc." And a mushroom omelet."

"Certainly, madame," he said, smiling at me. "Right away."

I was totally absorbed in the scene in front of me. The square was surrounded by cafes and shops, with an outdoor art exhibit in the middle. I watched people poking around among the paintings, some pretty good, some not. Lots of pictures of the Sacré Coeur, Notre Dame, the Eiffel Tower. Souvenir paintings to take home. My table was close to the narrow path that circled the square so I could hear snatches of German, French, English, Italian. A man stopped at my table, blocking my view.

"Want some company?" he said.

It was Ken, the keyboard guy from the Bateau Mouche.

"Oh hello," I said, surprised to see him. "What are you doing here?"

"I heard you tell your friends that you were coming up here, so I decided to follow you. Do you mind?"

"Of course I don't mind," I said. And I really

didn't. He seemed like a good guy and I wanted somebody to talk to. "Come sit with me." He pulled a chair over to my table and sat down next to me.

"When I saw you from across the square just now, you looked sad," he said. "Are you sad?"

"Not seriously," I said. "I was just remembering my honeymoon here."

He looked disappointed. "You're married?" he asked.

"Not anymore. I don't have much luck with husbands. But the honeymoon was great."

"How many husbands have you had?" he asked.

"Three," I said. "Either I have lousy taste in men or a short attention span."

"I know what you mean," Ken said. "I was married once."

"What happened?" I asked.

"She didn't want to live in Paris. Once I came here, I never wanted to leave. She wanted to stay in Baltimore. I kept coming back here for longer and longer visits, and finally I just stopped going home. She got a divorce. No hard feelings. She comes to see me in Paris once in a while"

"What is it about this city?" I asked him.

"It's so beautiful for one thing," he said. "Everywhere you go, there's something that takes your breath away. And French people are so different from Americans. Their whole attitude is: 'If you like me, fine. If you don't, who cares?' And I love the food and playing on the Bateau Mouche." He looked at me and smiled. "And meeting you. You're so lovely. You belong in Paris."

"Thank you, Ken," I said. "I do feel at home here. One of the places I loved was a little boîte near Sacré Coeur called the Lapin Agile. "The best musicians played there. We used to sit on the floor because it was always crowded and click our fingers instead of clapping. It was so cool. I don't suppose it's still there."

"Oh yeah," Ken said. "It's still there. It's famous all over the world. Sort of a legend. They always have the best musicians. It's still cool. Want to go there tonight?"

"Ask me again later," I said. "Let me see how I feel after dancing."

"You got it," he said.

The waiter brought my wine and omelet and Ken ordered a beer.

"Tell me about the people in your band and Monsieur Fouchet and Suzette and Madame Fouchet." I said. "Is there a little je ne sais quoi going on with Monsieur and Suzette, or is my imagination working overtime?"

"No, your imagination is right on target. Henri is fooling around with Suzette. I think Madame Fouchet knows it and ignores it. But they seem to have a whole different attitude toward cheating here. They don't take it as seriously as we do. It's just sex. As long as he doesn't screw her in public, Madame puts up with a little fooling around on the side. Besides, she's no angel either."

"No kidding," I said. "Who is she getting it on with?"

"Jean. You know, the trumpet player. I think she's more serious about him than he is about her though. He told me she talked about leaving her husband for him."

"Isn't he a little young for her?"

"They don't care about that over here," Ken said. "Did you see that Catherine Deneuve movie? *On My Way*, I think it's called. She sleeps with a really young guy and he says to her the next morning, 'You must have been really something when you were young.' She wasn't offended at all. I mean, it's a whole different way of looking at sex over here."

"How old are you?" I asked.

"Thirty-five," he said. "You?"

"Older," I said.

He raised his glass. "Here's to older," he said.

"Is Suzette in love with Monsieur Fouchet?" I asked.

"I think Suzette is in love with Suzette," Ken said.

"So we have stumbled into a romantic intrigue," I said. "Fascinating."

"Can't wait to see you Hoofers dance tonight. You were really terrific this morning at the rehearsal."

"Thanks." I looked at my watch. "I'd better go. I've got to dress and put on a ton of makeup and get back to the bateau by seven. I'm glad you followed me, Ken. Maybe you can show me your Paris."

"It would be my pleasure," he said.

I paid and left my keyboard guy people-watching at the cafe and took the Metro back to our apartment.

Everyone was there except Gini, who tends to lose track of time when she's taking photos.

Mary Louise and Tina showed me what they bought on the Champs-Élysées. A black silk blouse with tiny gold buttons for Mary Louise and a gorgeous blue and green scarf for Tina that looked fantastic with her bluer than blue eyes. They were the first thing you noticed when you met her.

"Can you believe this is a Dior scarf!" she said. "It was marked down to half its original price. Even in euros, it's a bargain."

"Oh Tina, it's gorgeous," I said. "I want one. How long is the sale going on?"

"Til the end of July, but you'd better hurry. The store was packed with shoppers. Lots of Parisians as well as tourists."

Pat was already in the shower. A good thing since all five of us had to use that one shower.

"Are we wearing black tonight?" I asked Tina.

"Yes, the skinny, clinging long dresses that are

cut down to our navels in front and up to our thighs on the sides."

"How do we get back to the boat in those things?" I asked. "Not the Metro, I hope?"

"No, no, Jan. Monsieur Fouchet is sending a car for us. Hurry up and get ready."

Pat came out wrapped in a towel and scooted into her room to get dressed.

We all managed to grab a quick shower and squeeze into our black slinky dresses, high-heeled tap shoes and rhinestone drop earrings by the time Gini appeared, fifteen minutes before the car was due to pick us up.

"Sorry, Tina," she said. "I meant to get back sooner." She looked so happy, it was hard to believe she was even a little bit sorry.

"Fifteen minutes, Gini," Tina said. "There's a car coming for us."

"Piece of cake," Gini said and shed her clothes and camera on the way to the shower. Twelve minutes later she was clean, made up and dressed. I could never do that.

On the dot of 6:45, a long black limo appeared and whisked us off to the Pont de l'Alma and our bateau. The French don't fool around with time. Once Derek and I were five minutes late for a bus tour full of French people, seated and waiting to start the tour. When we got on the bus, they all made a small disapproving noise—sort of a "Tsk, Tsk." We were never late again.

Inside, the boat was decorated with red, white and blue French flags everywhere on and around the white cloth-covered tables. The waiters stopped what they were doing to admire us as we stepped onto the boat. I must admit we were pretty gorgeous that night. I love it when people, mostly men, look at us like that, as if we were the most desirable women anywhere, any time, any place.

At the front of the bateau, the musicians wearing white jackets and pants, looked almost respectable. Suzette was fluttering around, flipping through the music sheets, humming a little, practically coming out of her thin-strapped, red, very short dress. She waved to us as we approached.

Madame Fouchet was talking to a man we hadn't seen before. He was tall, good-looking in an American kind of way—you know, toned and tanned, dark-haired, gray at the temples. Somewhere in his early fifties, I'd say.

She motioned to us to join them. "The Americans have arrived, I see," she said. "Allo, Hoofers. This is Alan Anderson, who owns a nightclub in New York, which he calls the Bateau Mouche. It's a *succés fou* with Americans. He wants to make it even more French by stealing away our Suzette to sing there. I just told him he couldn't have her. We need her here."

"Looking fine there, Hoofers," Anderson said, shaking hands with each of us as Madame

Fouchet introduced us. "I've heard good things about you."

Tina smiled at him. "Thanks, Alan," she said.

"Madame," Tina said to Fouchet's wife. "Where is your husband?"

"He's up on deck making sure everything is ready for viewing the fireworks at eleven o'clock when we anchor near the Eiffel Tower. All the guests go up there and watch. It's *magnifique*."

"Yeah," Jean said. "Where is Henri? He's been up there a long time. I thought he'd be back down here by now. He was supposed to okay the program."

"Oh you know Henri," his wife said. "He's a perfectionist. He wants every detail on deck to be perfect. That's so important tonight on this holiday."

"Maybe I should go up there and see if he needs some help," Jean said.

"No, no," Madame said. "He likes to do it all himself. I tried to help him earlier but he shooed me away. Just leave him alone. He'll be down here soon." She turned away from Jean and the rest of us. "I'll check the tables."

She walked back to the main part of the boat, where guests were beginning to arrive and take their seats. Mostly older people—the women dressed in long gowns and the men in dinner jackets—who could afford this expensive evening, they were escorted to their tables. Everyone seemed primed to enjoy this holiday celebration, and I was thrilled to be a part of it. I sneaked a peek at the menu for that night.

The appetizers were a choice of foie gras with a balsamic reduction and sea salt; avocado tartare with citrus and vitelotte potato chips; smoked Atlantic salmon with lemon and heavy cream; beef carpaccio, parmesan shavings, and bouquet of mesclun; and albacore tuna steak, sautéed roseval potatoes, drizzled with vinegar.

For the main course you could have fillet of French sea bream with roasted peaches and seasonal vegetables; prawns marinated in espelette chilies, and a vegetable trio; slow cooked lamb roast with a rosemary sauce; stuffed poultry tournedos, tomato mozzarella gratin; or zucchini cannelloni with vegetables, tomato, and pesto sauce.

Next you had a "duet of seasonal cheeses."

Then for dessert you were offered a dark chocolate tart (always my choice); iced strawberry meringue "vacherin"; yuzu cheesecake with berries; raspberry chocolate dome, passion fruit coulis; or chocolate speculoos cookies. I had no idea what half these things were—especially the yuzu cheesecake. I asked one of the waiters who spoke English what yuzu was, and even though he was rushing around making sure everything was perfect, he said, "It's a cross between a grapefruit and an orange—it's from Asia somewhere."

To accompany all this they gave you a bottle of wine for two people, with a choice of blanquette de Limoux AOC Castel Mouche; Vieilles vignes de l'Amiral; Lussac St. Emilion, AOC; Bourgogne Aligate, La Chablisienne.

I definitely planned to come back here as a passenger.

As the waiters brought the guests Kir Royales to drink while they waited for their appetizers, the boat slipped out of the harbor, smoothly gliding along the Seine past the exquisitely illuminated Grand Palais, under the Pont des Invalides, the Pont Alexandre III, under the Pont de la Concorde, where there were gasps of delight at the sight of the obelisk, the fountain and the ferris wheel all golden on this warm summer night.

We came out and bowed to our audience as the Bateau moved along past the Louvre. The band played the first strains of "Les Grands Boulevards," and Suzette's husky voice sang of the wide avenues of Paris with their booths and bazaars, the street vendors, so much to see, people out late on summer nights enjoying the sights and noises and joys of the most beautiful city on earth.

As she sang, we did our own tap dance down the grand boulevards of Paris. Shuffling, shim-shamming, time-stepping, high kicking, and grapevining, with some ball changes thrown in, we made that bateau our own. The dance floor at the front of the boat was just big enough for us to move the way we wanted to. We really got into it, the way we always do when the music is good and the mood sublime. Suzette's voice grew huskier and sexier as she repeated the first part of the song. Our legs kicked higher and our arms spread wider as we matched her love of Paris on this most festive of all nights of the year.

When we finished, the crowd applauded, cheered in several languages, clinked their knives against their glasses and cried, "Encore," "More," "Bravo."

We backed away until we were standing next to the band. We discreetly mopped our faces and bodies, which were shiny from dancing in 78-degree-heat in a small space. Suzette accepted a glass of champagne from Claude. He pulled her closer to him and whispered something in her ear. She closed her eyes and swayed a little. I thought she was going to faint, but she straightened up, shook her head and picked up another sheet of music.

"Want to do 'Padam' after the fireworks, Hoofers?" she asked. "That will give you enough time to dry off and catch your breath."

"That's fine, Suzette," Tina said. "But I really should check this with Monsieur Fouchet. I was sure he'd be here by now."

"He'll turn up soon," Suzette said, exchanging a look with Madame Fouchet. "*N'est-ce pas*, Madeleine?"

"Of course," Madame Fouchet said. "We won't be going up on deck to see the fireworks until the guests have had their dinner. He's probably just having a cigarette before he comes down. Don't worry."

The Bateau Mouche sailed slowly along the rest of the route, past the Hotel de Ville, Notre Dame, the Musée d'Orsay, the Palais Bourbon, and Les Invalides, all glowing golden against the night sky, as dinner was served. The waiters brought us a platter with a taste of all the courses, which were perfection.

Just as the guests were sipping the last of their coffee, the bateau stopped in front of the Eiffel Tower, where the fireworks were about to begin.

Jean stepped forward and the crowd stopped talking to listen to him.

"Monsieurs et mesdames," he said. "It is time for the piece de resistance of our holiday cruise. Please go up on deck and take the seats that we have provided for you. The fireworks will commence in fifteen minutes."

The guests pushed back their chairs and started up the stairs leading to the open deck on top of the bateau.

When the first two people stepped onto the deck, there was a loud scream. An American woman with white hair started back down the steps. "There's a man up there," she said. "I think he's dead! There's blood all over."

Jean pushed his way through the crowd on the stairs and said, "Will you return to your seats, please, ladies and gentlemen. You will be able to see the fireworks through the windows below."

"Are you kidding?" the woman said. "I don't want to stay on this boat another moment. How can you talk about fireworks with a dead man lying there?" She turned to her companion, an elderly gentleman who didn't seem to understand what was going on.

"What's the matter, Elyse?" he said. "Why did you scream like that?"

"Never mind, Andrew," she said. "Let's just get out of here."

Madame Fouchet quickly reached the woman's side, patted her arm and said in a soothing voice, "Please sit down, madame. We will be back at the dock in a few minutes and you will be able to leave the boat then."

She clapped her hands together and said to the head waiter, "Paul, brandy for everyone, *s'il vous plaît.*"

Elyse and Andrew returned reluctantly to their seats as did the other passengers. The cheerful mood of the evening had vanished. Even the free brandy didn't help.

I grabbed Jean when he came back down the stairs. "What's happened, Jean? Who is it?"

He pulled me over to the side. "It's Henri. He's dead. It looks like he was shot. I've got to call the police."

He pulled out his phone and went to the front of the boat where he told the other members of the band, my gang and Suzette what had happened.

Suzette didn't say anything. She just stood there looking stunned, clinging to the cellist, Claude.

Jean was dialing the police when Madame Fouchet ran over to him and took the phone away from him. She said something to him in French. He started to argue with her, but she prevailed and prevented him from dialing.

Since the whole conversation was in French, I had no idea what she was saying, or why she wouldn't let Jean call the police. From the look on Gini's face I could tell there was something odd going on. Tina and I pulled her over to the side next to Pat and Mary Louise.

"What's going on, Gini?" Tina said. "Could you hear what she said?"

"Yeah," Gini said, speaking in a low voice. "It makes no sense. Madame Fouchet told Jean not to phone the police until all the passengers were off the boat. She didn't want them to be questioned. She said it would be bad publicity for the bateau and nobody would sail on it again."

"That's crazy," Pat said. "You mean, all these people are just going to disappear without the police talking to them to find out if they saw anything suspicious? One of them might even have killed him. It makes no sense."

"Looks that way," Gini said.

"If she's not going to call the police, one of us should," Tina said.

We all looked at Gini. "Hey, not me," she said, shaking her head.

"You have to," Tina said. "You're the only one who speaks French well enough to explain what happened."

"You're right, Tina," Gini said. "You're always right." She reached for her phone. "Allo," she said, but before she could continue, a man's hand took her phone away. "I've already called them, Gini," Alan Anderson, the American nightclub owner said.

I was surprised to see him because I hadn't noticed him at any of the tables when we were dancing.

"Are you mad?" Madame Fouchet said to him when she realized what he had done. "You have ruined our business."

"Madeleine," Anderson said to her in low, carefully modulated tones, "They tell you your husband is lying up there on the deck, obviously murdered by someone on this boat, and you haven't even gone up there to see if it's really him. And you want to let everybody off the boat before anyone is questioned? Do you want everyone to think you put business before your husband? Or even that you might be the one who killed him?"

Madame Fouchet's expression changed from angry to chastened.

"Oh Alan, you're right, of course. I wasn't thinking clearly. Take me up there, will you please. I can't do it alone."

He took her hand and led her up the stairs to the upper deck just as the bateau pulled into the dock, where we could see the police waiting to board her.

Catering and Capers with
Isis Crawford!

Grab These Cozy Mysteries
from
Kensington Books